DESTINATION PREMEDITATION

DESTINATION PREMEDITATION
a horror novella
by Sandy Lender

IYF Publishing/Dragon Hoard Press

IYF Publishing/Dragon Hoard Press
Florida
USA

This is a work of fiction. Names, characters, places, and incidents are products of the author's imagination or are used fictitiously and are not to be construed as real. Any resemblance to actual events, locales, organizations, or persons, living or dead, is entirely coincidental.

First edition published in USA, 2020.
Print ISBN 978-1-7345152-5-1
Cover design by Sandy Lender
Cover image courtesy of Art Tower of Pixabay

Dedication

To all the Duranies who travel,
and who have crammed
eight or twelve people into one hotel room ...

Acknowledgments

Thank you to "brigwer" for the unlimited creative use of the cover image. It's wonderfully creepy and perfect. I wish I could have bought you more coffee.

Thank you to Wendy for going with me to Smokehouse to discuss what plot devices were going to offend readers the most. I think I toned them down.

A big thank-you goes out to the other writers who participate in The International 3-Day Novel Contest, where this story began in 2019, and to the multitude of travelers through the Tampa International Airport who have provided character studies over the years.

Prologue

The interior decorator didn't know Mrs. Molly Powell personally, but she figured the elderly caretaker of Manatee Moss Hidden Manor would not approve of the party raging on the first floor. Granted, the contractor Mrs. Powell had hired to update the manor for the upcoming season had done an exemplary job modernizing the estate, but that didn't give the crew the right to wreck the place now. The ruckus downstairs would leave Josie's employees little time to clean up before the first guests from the Airbnb site would show up expecting a clean, WiFi-on-the-inside, Crystal River experience.

One could say the party happened at the wrong time, in the wrong place.

The workmen smashing glass Modelo bottles against the newly installed hardwood floor in the kitchen and dining room were making the kind of disrespectful mess that Mrs. Powell would not abide. Or so Josie assumed. She had a feeling the sour-faced woman with the too-tight gray bun on the back of her head wouldn't go in for a game of beer pong on the polished oak dining room table.

She didn't think Mrs. Powell would give them "credit" for containing the party to the left side of the house, either. No, the unsettling stench of peyote and a couple different varieties of marijuana snaked through the halls and air vents and up the staircase where Josie hung curtains in one of the guest rooms. It occurred to her that the curtains—and bedding—might have to be re-washed after this ridiculous night if the crew didn't knock it off. Hopefully, the amount of drugs passing around the kitchen would sicken the men into going home. Seriously, if the smoke was thick enough to make her feel light-headed clear up here in the egret room, how sickly must the users be feeling?

Her smartwatch told her it was closing in on midnight.

"No wonder I'm exhausted," she muttered, dragging a folding stepstool to the window. She depressed and held the button to release the lock and unfolded the mini ladder in front of the window, settling it, giving it a bit of a shake to check its stability, and then straightened to see her reflection in the darkness of a Central Florida night. Beyond the glass, a banyan tree surrounded by palms, cypress, oak, and crepe myrtle silhouetted against a partly cloudy sky. Not a bad night at all for late October. Not a bad night at all.

Except the night had an obnoxious polka tuba shaking the walls and floor on a persistent two-four beat.

She collected the curtain rod, heavy with the two panels she gathered in the center to keep from tripping on them, and brought the mass of material and metal to the window. As she leaned to step onto the stool, a streak of red across the glass caught her eye. Something higher than the ground, but lower than the treetops, had a light that mimicked her own reflection. When she tried to focus on it, she saw nothing but herself, holding yards of egret-white material, looking at black and gray night.

Luckily, the effects of hallucinatory smoke are easy to shrug off.

As she lifted the weighty curtain rod up, above her head, into place on its brackets, exposing her torso to the darkness beyond the glass, the music downstairs ceased. A sudden, blessed stillness blanketed the night. No more shaking. No more rattling. She didn't realize how the constant sound had been hammering against her brain until its absence sucked the oppression away. Like the seal formed when closing the windows in a speeding car, she felt fingers against her eardrums, forcing her to swallow. In fact, the fingers began to squeeze harder. The physical force pushed into her brain as if she'd been plunged into more than silence; plunged into some kind of tunnel that ended in the glass before her.

The window cracked under the pressure.

Josie shrieked, but no one came to her rescue. Her body bent forward as if someone pulled her hips toward the fracturing glass. Sudden shards of window pieces exploded inward, shredding her body as she broke outward, raking her skin like many dozen jagged knives until she hung, folded, suspended in time and space above the second story while her blood drained, drained, drained to feed the sandy soil far below. Gasping for air with which to scream burned not just her lungs, but also the exposed muscle and tissue around them. Josie blinked at the stars above, her mind trying to grasp the signals coming in from broken bones, broken skin, broken life. With a final available breath, she forced a prayer upward, toward the stars.

The invisible claw released her to fall, hitting the ground in a crumpled mass of broken bone and shredded skin.

Chapter 1

Pre-holiday travelers swarmed Tampa International Airport. Their range of autumn attire entertained Laurel; she almost laughed at a woman carrying an honest-to-God parka toward the Goddard elevators before she reminded herself the gal *could* be returning from a northern visit. Just because someone entered Florida a week before Thanksgiving didn't mean the person was vacationing.

The Gulf Coast still boasted muggy temperatures with highs in the eighties; a majority of the chunky tourists sweated and swore as they lugged their carry-ons past Laurel's mound of real estate in baggage claim. While a businessman huffed past her with a rain slicker in one hand and beat-up roller bag bouncing behind him toward the green elevators, Laurel sat back in her chair and disturbed her traveling companion with, "Hey."

Jackie moaned from under a floppy straw hat.

"Did you bring a raincoat or umbrella?" Laurel asked her.

The straw hat turned and tilted as Jackie moved to look from under it. Aquamarine eyes that could have been set in a Disney princess character peeked at Laurel. Jackie could captivate a Disney prince—or a Tolkien king—with those baby blues, even when half asleep. "It's November."

"Right. Jen said it wouldn't rain this time a'year, but I just saw a dude with a raincoat thing in his hand. Like he knew what he was doing."

"Going to these green elevators?" Jackie asked.

"Mmm-hmm. They buggin' you?" Laurel teased.

"Naw. I just can't figure out the naming convention around here. Janis. Goddard. Are we supposed to know what these words mean?"

Laurel smiled at her girlfriend, not condescending, but kind. It wasn't surprising that Jackie didn't recognize the less-widely-known names of heroes of flight—schools were hardly sharing positive history of the United States any longer. "Robert Hutchings Goddard was a rocket scientist," she said. "He launched the first liquid-fired rocket like a hundred years ago."

"A big deal, then?" Jackie asked.

"Yep. A big deal. He's considered a founding father of modern rocketry."

Jackie offered a sideward smile at her then, her baby blues filled with admiration. "You *would* know this, my own Hidden Figure."

Laurel's vascular response sent a warm rush to her cheeks and forehead, heating her face under Jackie's sincere adoration. Jackie responded by resuming the napping position, her blonde bob tickling her chin as she nodded forward.

Laurel resumed people-watching. That public activity goes both ways, though. Some of the travelers who walked past the ladies stared at them. Jackie wasn't noticing because she napped under her hat, but Laurel saw them staring and she let her mind conjure little worries.

She wondered if they stared because Jackie was a beautiful blonde bombshell and Laurel considered herself plain. She considered her hair too frizzy and her skin too dark, no matter how many times Jackie told her she was an African queen. Laurel had always thought of them as mis-matched.

Or did tourists stare because she'd propped against the mound of luggage a sign that read "Bend and Neil Wedding." Laurel grinned at one fellow who tripped over his feet as he went by, staring. When her phone chimed, she had to stop entertaining herself with what people might be thinking.

"Tell me that's Marigold," Jackie moaned.

"Hopefully she's not here already," Laurel said, bringing up the text screen. "Kandy's flight doesn't land for another couple minutes and you know she's got a full ton of luggage to get...What the hell?"

The straw hat tilted again. "That sounds ominous."

"Listen to this."

The phone chimed again before Laurel could begin reading.

"Marigold's got a fitting and some kind of bridesmaid thing with the girls, so she's not picking us up. She's sending Brad."

Jackie moaned her displeasure. "Not Clara?"

"Doesn't say. Just says, 'was sending Brad to drive the van.'"

"That'll be a laugh a minute."

"But wait," Laurel put on her game-show-host voice for a second. "There's more. Brad isn't feeling well."

The phone chimed again and again while Laurel read off the messages, paraphrasing the emoticons and gifs for her girlfriend.

"Brad's vomiting so he's staying in bed. We have to get an Uber."

"From here to Crystal River? Why can't Clara drive the van? She's a big girl."

"Says Brad won't let her leave the kids."

"Wait."

Jackie sat up fully and pulled off the straw hat. Her tousled bob fell back into place as she spoke with plenty of gesturing.

"You're telling me Clara brought that jackass *and* her two kids, but none of the three adults who said they'd pick us up are actually coming to pick us up? And they're telling us this at the time they were supposed to be here to get us?"

"Looks that way."

Jackie put her finger and thumb to either side of the bridge of her nose and squeezed, closing her eyes against the angst rising around her. "Fine. We'll rent another car. There are four of us meeting here in the next few minutes, right?"

"I don't know which would be cheaper. Rent a car for a week or Uber back and forth."

"Hey, guys!" someone yelled, waving a phone as she approached them and their wedding sign.

Laurel politely rose to hug the newcomer. "Taryn. It's good to see you in person."

"Ditto. Did you get copied on the text about our ride?" the gal asked, pulling one earbud from one ear. As if she expected breaking news, she left the other earbud in place behind stringy blonde hair falling out of a messy ponytail.

"Apparently, yes," Jackie said.

"Suckage, right?" This newcomer, Taryn, with overly large smile, seemed to be taking the change in plans in stride. "I wish I'd known sooner because I could have arranged for a car to meet us here when we got our bags, but I can get one now. Are we ready to go?"

"We're waiting for Kandy," Laurel said.

"We haven't decided what to do," Jackie said. "An Uber might be more expensive than renting another car."

Taryn tilted her head to the side, similar to a confused puppy, and widened the already toothy smile. "I mean, our group has the van and a four-door already, right? So-oh, if we rent another car, that will be three vehicles for twelve people. That might be a lot. If that's what everyone *else* wants to do, I'm totally fine with it, of course, but it might be overkill. Taking a ride-share up to Crystal River one way won't be as expensive as renting a third car for five days. Should we call Marigold and see if *she* thinks that's the best way to go?"

Jackie stared at the young woman, unable to form a polite response.

"I don't think Marigold will care what we do," Laurel said. "But I agree taking a ride-share one way won't be as bad as taking it both ways."

"Great," Taryn said. "I'll use the app on my phone to get us a car. How long do you think it'll be before Kandy's ready?"

Jackie replaced her hat, pulling it down over her eyes as she leaned back in the chair. Laurel understood this sign; her girlfriend needed space.

Laurel smiled politely at Taryn. "She was supposed to land at 2:31. Terminal A."

"Gotcha. Do you care if I get us a car from Lyft instead of Uber? I heard you say Uber, but I would have to re-install the Uber app on my phone. I just prefer Lyft because I think they treat their drivers better."

Laurel sensed Jackie vibrating with irritation behind her. "I think Lyft would be fine," Laurel answered.

"Great," Taryn said again. "I'll check the arrivals for Kandy's plane and line up a car for us. Can I leave my carry-on here with you guys?"

"Of course. Add it to the mass here."

When Laurel sat back down, Jackie leaned a bit toward her and said, "It's thirteen people on wedding day."

"What?" Laurel asked.

"Taryn just told us three cars for twelve people would be too much, but the little brainiac must've forgot Marigold's boytoy is joining us on the day of the wedding. That'll make us a baker's dozen trudging around Crystal River looking for the beach. And then we'd be in four cars because he's driving over. So-oh, you know, I mean."

Laurel couldn't help giggling. "You can*not* mock her all week. You'll kill me."

"Understood, Captain. But she's already worse in person than on Zoom. You may have to keep her away from me. The two-hour drive coming up? I need to be placed in a coma so I can sleep and ignore all that's going on."

"I'll tell everyone to let you sleep," Laurel said.

"And you know we're gonna end up living at this airport on the way home, right? Getting a rental car would've been the way to go."

"Prob'ly. But I figure a week from now, we can rent a car to drop off at the airport for a day or whatever and it'll be, what, thirty bucks? By the time we get to the end of this vacation, I think you'll be ready to pay thirty bucks for that privacy and convenience."

"I'm ready to pay it right now," Jackie moaned. "I've over-peopled for the day and we're not even at the house yet."

Chapter 2

At an antebellum-style house mostly obscured by palm and cypress trees, palmetto bushes, and nature-directed hedgerows of bramble, six members of the November Wedding Extraordinaire had already "checked into" the Airbnb. Marigold Koure, one of Jen Neil's bridesmaids, had made the reservation, and had taken possession of the property Tuesday, about the time the Brandon family had arrived.

The house looked freshly painted in a non-offensive beige with darker beige shutters and banisters accenting its southern-inspired accoutrements, but held a darker, oak interior. Polished wood running boards and banisters inside reflected recessed lighting but couldn't quite cut the darkness of the place. All curtains had to be open and all lights on to chase away shadows and give a person a true appreciation for the detail in the floral wallpaper and grain of the wood flooring.

Truly a gorgeous home at one time, the mansion had been restored to serve a fiduciary purpose without giving up its beauty.

Deep into day two and bordering on a migraine, Clara Brandon already washed a load of her family's clothes in the utility area of the kitchen. Someone had cleverly built a closet with accordion wooden doors against the inner wall that shared the downstairs washroom; while it fit nicely in the space, it warmed the already warm room to the point Clara needed to fan herself with a paper plate.

Standing in front of the washer, watching the tiny square under the word "spin" blink red and clear, red and clear, red and clear, she tried to remember where she could find the circuit breaker for the room. This was obviously the electrical center of the house, even if located in a back corner logistically.

Washer, dryer, two blessed coffee makers plus an espresso machine, toaster oven, microwave oven, some kind of water filtration system, garbage disposal—she'd lost count of the extra amenities when reading about the place online. Now that she stood beside a twenty-one-cubic-foot refrigerator, she lost count again. The noise from the washer wasn't helping her concentration.

Despite the newness of the machine, its spin cycle sounded like a lumberjack losing his battle with one of the trees outside. Outside and nearby. The uneven thwacks had no rhythm to them but did have a pounding effect on Clara's head.

"Mom!"

Clara whipped around to face her daughter, ignoring the pinch in the lower portion of her spine as she did so.

"Jesus, Mary, and Joseph, Penny. What's wrong with you, sneaking up on me like that?"

"I've been here for like ten minutes," the child lied.

"I don't think that's true, young lady. What do you need?"

"I wanna go swimming. Patrick wants to, too. Where's my suit?"

"No, not today. Put on a movie in your room. Not too loud."

The child must not have believed her final answer because Clara didn't put enough energy into it. There was no shaking of her head—due to the building migraine.

"But we wanna swim out back."

"No. You can't swim without adult supervision and I'm getting chores done before the rest of our friends get here."

The little girl rolled her eyes, which Clara had found a difficult habit to break in a five-year-old. Knowing Penny's propensity for disobedience, Clara glanced at the child-lock on the kitchen door—the lock designed and installed to comply with Florida codes to protect naughty toddlers from sneaking into pool areas.

"What's adult supervision anyway?" Penny asked.

"It means you need your mom or your dad to keep you safe, and your dad isn't feeling well right now."

"Why can't Grandpa watch us?"

"You know why Grandpa Brandon can't watch you swim. Do you want to take a sandwich out front to him? He'd probably like to have a visit from you to interrupt his afternoon."

Penny screwed up her face to show she hated that idea. "I think Dad could watch us from the window."

"I told you, your dad isn't feeling well right now. He can't watch you. There's a button on the remote for the channel with the shows you like."

Penny made a clucking sound with the front of her tongue. "Dad's never feeling well."

"Don't be a rude girl. Would you rather help me make tuna salad? You can help me peel all those eggs. We can do it together."

Penny chose to go the movie route by turning on her heel and marching through the open doorway into the enormous front dining room.

Unlike the puzzle-piece second story, the house wasn't difficult to navigate downstairs. A person could run laps through the kitchen and dining room, across the front entryway, around the staircase, and up the hallway that passed the fancy rooms on the right-hand side of the house, and around the back of the staircase where another passthrough led to the kitchen again.

Easy.

The two children, aged five and three, had put it to the test Tuesday night until they were red in the face and exhausted. As were their parents.

"Put on a movie for you and Patrick until our friends get here," Clara called after her. "It should be soon."

From the other side of the kitchen, her husband spoke next. "You people have no clue how to be quiet."

Clara whipped around to face him, and this time, couldn't ignore the pinch in the lower portion of her spine. She grabbed her lower back as she said, "Jesus, Mary, and Joseph. You scared the life out of me."

"Yeah, well, you're always jumpy. When are they getting here?"

"Laurel's Uber should arrive within the next fifteen minutes or so. Give or take. She texted me they were on Highway 98, which I think is the one—"

"Yeah, yeah, yeah. I get it. Fifteen minutes. And the people coming from Orlando?"

"Probably half an hour. They were waiting on Sue's flight to—"

"Got it. Everyone's getting here *soon*. I'm gonna run to the liquor store to get some beers and stuff for tonight."

"But you're sick. You can't go out looking for a store the way you're feeling."

"I'm a registered driver on the van, so, yes, I can," he argued. The way he squinted his jaundiced eyes against not-at-all bright light in the kitchen belied his driving abilities. "I'll be right back."

"Marigold needs the van to go for her fitting. She has an appointment at five and—"

He put a ball cap on his thin, greasy hair and scowled at her. "Did you not hear me? I said, I'll be right back. And she can take the car they're bringing from Orlando, right? Stop freaking out."

Clara couldn't stop him. Even if she wanted to confront him, her six-foot-tall husband had seven inches of height and eight years of anger on her. She couldn't match him. The randomly banging washer slowed to a halt and began a chiming tune that didn't sound like any particular song. It clicked to signal unlocking and she yanked the lid open to stop the dinging chant.

Chapter 3

The Lyft driver reached the Crystal River area ninety minutes after the four-member gang departed the Tampa airport. Trees in various shades of green with all types of fronds and leaves hung over the highway at one point, giving Laurel the sense that she had left civilization behind. This was the swamp land she imagined when dreaming of a vacation in Florida. It was Everglade-like yet civilized enough to have a paved road on which a human could drive a seven-passenger Kia© Sedona.

"That one was nice," Kandy said, pointing as the minivan on which Laurel focused went by. "I hope they rented a van like that one. Lotsa room." It wasn't surprising that a mom-of-a-toddler appreciated the roominess of a large minivan.

"No kidding," Laurel agreed. "And a pretty blue. You know, we're kinda in the middle of nowhere, Benjamin. Is the GPS still guiding us?"

"I'm still getting a signal," Taryn said, as if someone had spoken to her in the past hour.

"Yes, ma'am," the driver answered. "We're turning on this road...right...up...here."

He slowed to signal and make a turn where Laurel could swear the minivan had come from. And that set her mind at ease. More civilization and tourist destinations meant more security. Benjamin was less likely to take them to a deserted swamp area to kill and dump them if other drivers were using the roads they traversed.

Of course, the sense of ease dissipated the further he drove into the vegetation. He finally turned onto a one-lane, gravel road with potholes that could have eaten the mid-size SUV. Jackie could no longer pretend to be asleep. The jostling bounced her head off the window and brought the four women to whining attention.

"This is crazy," Jackie muttered.

"Are you sure this is the right way?" Laurel asked.

As a splash of beige came into view behind the green trees, the driver pointed toward it. "Manatee Moss Hidden Manor," he said.

"Hidden is a fact," Kandy said. She took the final minute of travel to pull her lush brown hair into a ponytail, securing it with a green scrunchie that matched her green t-shirt.

Within the next thirty seconds, Benjamin drove into a clearing that represented the driveway and parking lot for the house. They gaped at its massive wrap-around porch and newly painted columns holding up an ornately decorated upper balcony.

"Where's the other cars?" Kandy asked.

"This has to be the right place," Taryn said. "We drove right to the address. And it looks like the picture on the website, just a different color. More updated."

"Yep," Laurel agreed. "There's Clara."

They saw their middle-aged friend step onto the porch and wave. She stopped next to an older man in a rocking chair, placing her plump hand on his shoulder.

"Omigod, she brought her dad to this?" Jackie said. "I assume that's her dad?"

"Looks like. Why's the van missing?" Kandy repeated.

"It's prob'ly around back or something," Jackie said.

"Do you see a way to get to the back of this place?" Kandy asked.

"I mean, guys, this looks adorable, even with the spooky swamp-forest vibe, okay?" Taryn said. "Let's be positive. And, remember, Marigold had an appointment for wedding stuff, so she probably took the van to that."

"And the others aren't here from Orlando yet?" Kandy asked.

"Exactly. They're on their way, same as us," Laurel chimed in.

As if he was ready to dump them out and be on his way, the driver looked at Kandy in the seat next to him and said, "That's two hundred bucks."

"What?" Taryn balked. "Back at the airport, you said it was one-fifty. The app should be charging me one-fifty, as agreed."

"Tolls," he said simply.

"Omigod, I'll pay the extra fifty," Jackie called from the back, "but you know that eats your tip."

"I figure," he groused.

"And you know you get the fifty *after* you get our stuff into the house," Jackie finished.

Laurel hid her grin from the driver, not wanting to antagonize the person who would be sloughing their belongings, but she appreciated Jackie's expression of angst. The driver was being rude; taking advantage.

Taryn collected her carry-on bag from the floorboard at her feet and slung it over her shoulder as she popped out of the second row of bucket seats. "I got mine. I fit everything into this one bag. It's got a ton of pockets to keep things organized inside. It's ahh-mazing. I really wanted to keep things compact so I wouldn't take up too much room in the van. I mean, I knew we were going to be cramming a bunch of us and all our stuff in there. And I wasn't sure what the space will be like in the house. I mean, it was so vague on Airbnb's site, you know? You can never tell what size rooms really are by those pictures. They're so misleading."

She turned to face the house.

"But this place is so much more than what it looks like on the site."

~ ~ ~

About half an hour after the women had arrived at the house, they were still gabbing and giggling in the front parlor with Clara and her two kids. They'd helped Mr. Brandon up to the room he shared with the children, so he didn't have to endure the silliness, and he seemed pleased to escape the noise, but they hadn't taken the time to move their bags anywhere yet. Clara took more headache medicine and brought extra toys down to keep Patrick and Penny occupied.

The entryway opened to either the dining room to the left or the parlor to the right, and the parlor had softer chairs and couches to lounge on. Lounging was preferable to unpacking. Catching up on life was better than labor at the moment, thus they were mid-uproar when Brad returned in the van.

Kandy had taken an overstuffed leather chair near the enormous front window and sat twirling a lock of hair that had escaped its ponytail while they talked. She was first to hear the crunch of gravel under tires.

"I hear them! Finally!" Kandy jumped up from her chair, thinking the friends from Orlando had arrived.

"Ugh," Laurel moaned. "I don't know if I can get back up off this couch to help them in. I'm stuck here."

"I'll second that," Jackie said. "I could sleep right here."

"You slept all the way here from the airport," Taryn said. "You should be up all night. My mom used to tell me that every fifteen minutes spent napping during the day would screw up an hour of sleep through the night."

"I'll risk it," Jackie said, winking at Laurel.

Brad swore as he opened the front door to the sight of luggage and purses piled up around the entry. "What's this mess? What's going on?"

"False alarm," Kandy announced, reclaiming her chair.

"Well, that's a fine hello," Brad said. "False alarm? What are you girls waiting on? Pizza delivery for a porno scene?"

"That's nice," Jackie muttered.

"We're watching for the girls from the other airport," Clara said.

"Well, I bought party beverages for everyone," he said. As if making his point, he set a case of beer and paper bag next to a suitcase.

"So-oh...too sick to drive to the airport to pick us up, but finding a liquor store for party supplies? No problem."

Jackie and Laurel exchanged amused glances at Taryn's pointed comment, but Clara didn't look amused at all. Her eyes went wide for a second, and then she laughed nervously. "Ah, that's funny, Taryn." She had risen from her chair with some discomfort from the pinch in her lower back, saying, "Here, let me help you."

"There's a wicked bad accident up at the corner to turn down this road," Laurel overheard him tell Clara. "Looks like it just happened. SUV flipped over. Completely totaled."

Kandy leaned toward Taryn's chair as the couple went back out, leaving the door open to facilitate bringing in more cases of whatever Brad had in the van. "I don't think it's a good idea to antagonize him," Kandy whispered.

"Yeah, my dad gets mad a lot," Penny agreed.

The women stared at the little girl for a second, unsure how to respond to a five-year-old who said such things. Then Penny made eye contact with Laurel specifically. The child lowered her chin a bit and lowered her voice almost an octave. She practically whispered, "but I think this house will cure him of his anger."

Laurel shivered.

"Wow," Jackie said. "Let's talk about something fun to do tomorrow."

As if she hadn't just channeled some kind of horror movie ghost, Penny's whole demeanor brightened and she said, "I want to go swimming tomorrow and I need adult supervision."

"I think we've been invited to swim," Kandy said.

"I'm not as old as everyone else here, but I'm adult enough to supervise," Taryn joked.

"How *did* you and Jen meet?" Jackie blurted out.

"Me?" Taryn asked.

"Yeah. Aren't you twenty years younger than the rest of us? We all met in college. Where did you and Jen meet?"

"I thought Marigold met Jen clear back in high school," Taryn corrected her. "But Jen and I work together. I just started at the shop this spring when I graduated. I was an intern there last year and Jen really helped me get things figured out."

Jackie nodded, satisfied with the answer.

"Hey, now I *know* I hear another car," Kandy said. "That's got to be them this time."

Her guess was backed up by the sound of a car honking repeatedly and someone hollering like a cowboy rounding up cattle outside.

"Yep. That'll be Becky right there," Laurel said.

The explosion of sound and energy took a while to bring under control. Clara shuffled her kids to the room they shared with their grandfather upstairs, but Brad was more interested in playing bartender to the remaining seven ladies. Becky lugged her bags up to the wolf room, which she'd have to herself, so she could make a quick call home before settling in with the gang.

At one point toward dusk, someone asked about Marigold, who was supposed to be staying at the house with them.

"She grabbed a cab to an event with the other bridesmaids tonight," Clara answered.

"Oh, yeah, and that's completely my fault," Brad began. Before he could launch his tirade, a pounding noise startled them.

A heavy rapping sounded against the kitchen window at the back of the house, bringing Kandy up out of her chair. The banging continued against the glass for several seconds, as if the person pre-emptively refused to be ignored.

"Holy crap," Jackie said. "Is someone breaking in?"

"I mean, is there an alarm we should've set?" Taryn asked. "It's not all that dark yet."

"No one's breaking in," Brad snapped. "I'll get the door."

From upstairs, Penny shouted down the open stairwell, "Mom! Something's trying to get in from the back porch!"

"It's okay, sweetie. Go back to your movie."

"Kay!"

"Wow, raising kids is easy," Jackie said, giving Laurel a wink.

Clara shook her head slightly. "Or at least it might be if anyone helped once in a while."

"You've got some helpers this weekend," Laurel said. "I think swimming is on the agenda for tomorrow?"

Clara smiled. "That would be great. Penny's been wanting to jump in that pool since we got here yesterday. We've been too crazy getting Brad's dad settled and getting the groceries and stuff for here."

"The groceries. That's what I was gonna thank you for next," Laurel said.

From the kitchen, they heard Brad start swearing.

Chapter 4

"That doesn't sound right," Jackie said, hopping to her feet.

"Jesus, Mary, and Joseph. What's going on?" Clara asked.

About then, Becky came clomping down the wooden staircase sounding like an unshod horse. "What's happening?" she asked.

"Someone's at the back door," Laurel answered.

Most of them were on their feet at this point, spurred by Brad's cursing-followed-by-silence, to investigate. But no one had to go beyond the foyer and staircase. He walked through the dining room with a much older woman matching his stride.

"This is the caretaker of the manor," Brad explained. "Miss Polly—"

"I'm Mrs. Molly Powell," she interrupted. Her ancient voice rasped as if she'd been smoking since her teens—a century or two ago. It was a voice long wearied of droning its disappointment with heathens and ne'er-do-wells. "Which of you is Marigold Koure?"

"Marigold is at a dinner thing tonight," Taryn answered. "She'll be back late. Can we give her a message for you?"

The woman's dark eyes bore into Taryn then, singling her out for evaluation. It struck them all as odd that she didn't wear glasses. A woman with that many wrinkles crinkling her eyes into scrunches surely couldn't see them clearly. What was she seeing when staring daggers at each person in the house she monitored?

"I need to confirm the contract with Marigold Koure. How many of you are here?"

A murmur in Laurel's brain whispered to her, compelling her to answer succinctly: "There are eleven adults and two children."

Mrs. Powell's piercing eyes took in Laurel for a second, then switched to Clara where the glare seemed to soften a measure. "Who are all these people?"

"Well, ah, mostly we're friends of the bride," Clara answered. "We're here for the wedding that Marigold is a part of. You just met my husband, Bradley Brandon. I'm Clara. Brad's father is upstairs with our two children."

Clara paused and Laurel obeyed the voice whispering in her head, and took up the narrative, "I'm Laurel Moreno." She gestured toward Jackie, sensing the need to be cautious in how she introduced her girlfriend. "This is Jaclyn Jones. This is Taryn Smith."

"You seem younger than these others," Mrs. Powell interrupted, boring her black gaze into Taryn again. "Are you the children's nanny?"

"I mean, sure, I'm not as old as these friends from college, but I'm one of the gang. I'm new to the group. I work with the bride."

Mrs. Powell re-focused her attention on Laurel. "Go on."

"Yes, ah, this is Kandice Moynihan. Becky Ellexen is on the step there. This is Harmony Ross and here's Susan Stein."

Mrs. Powell nodded slightly, taking in the names and faces as if memorizing this group of thirty- and forty-somethings. Since entering the foyer, she hadn't unfolded her hands from their tight, arthritic clasp. The way she signaled a change in attention was with that piercing, dark glare.

She stared at Sue for what felt like a full minute, making everyone uncomfortable, making them wonder what she was about to ask of the gal in a creatively baggy dress. Mrs. Powell offered Sue a sort of half-smile, half-sneer, and then shifted her gaze back to Clara.

"And Dorian? Marigold mentioned a man named Dorian Butcher. Where is he?"

"No one knows what Dorian's gonna do," Laurel said.

"He's Marigold's 'plus one,' but he might not make it for the wedding," Taryn said.

Mrs. Powell stiffened her neck, inhaling deeply before offering her decree. "That is acceptable. As the caretaker, I live in the cottage at the back of the property, near the dock. If there is anything you require during your stay, you may ring the bell at my door, and I will assist you as best I can.

"I encourage you to seek my permission before making any changes to the furniture arrangements or décor. It is in the contract Miss Koure agreed to that you will not damage or change anything in the house or on the grounds.

"You must be mindful of your trash and recycling items. There are labeled containers in a fenced area off the side of the lanai where you are to place your trash and recycling items. This area must be kept neat and orderly. I've discussed this with Miss Koure, of course, but I want to reiterate that it is important that you be respectful of the property.

"If you wish to move furniture from one room to another, you are to replace it before you depart Monday.

"You are still departing Monday, is that correct?"

Laurel confirmed their travel details while the rest of the group exchanged confused glances.

"Please remember to keep the kitchen neat and tidy during your stay. We have large insects that are attracted to crumbs and standing water in Florida. If you can keep the house clean and free of damage, there will be less chance of these insects being attracted to the house. Or to your belongings. You do not want to take anything *disturbing* home with you."

They all stared back at her. It seemed a strange visit. Laurel couldn't understand why this woman needed to lecture grown adults on how to behave in a guest house.

"If there is nothing you need at this time, I will return to my cottage," she said. "Please let Miss Koure know that I would like to speak with her in the morning."

"Of course," Laurel said.

"So-oh, maybe you *could* help with something," Taryn said, as if she suddenly remembered they had been making movie-night plans. "We need a mini HDMI cable to hook up to the TV in the living room." She pointed toward the front room they had all been in just moments before the strange visit.

Mrs. Powell stared into Taryn again, this time her scowl couldn't be mistaken for anything but annoyance. "I do not think I have an aychdee mye cable, mini or otherwise. I cannot help you. Please do not make any changes to the television set in the parlor."

"Oh, so, it's like a wire that goes from a device like a laptop so you can watch movies on TV. It's not anything that will mess up the TV. It's a cable, like a wire."

Mrs. Powell offered a tight grimace, giving Laurel the idea, her patience had reached its limit. "The workers who refurbished some of these rooms had many wires and cables left over. Some were placed in a box that is now stored in the attic. You may look there. If you choose to do so, be careful when accessing the attic as the flooring is old and not as sturdy as the rest of the house."

Taryn seemed overjoyed with the result of the conversation, but the rest of the group wanted to step away from the unsettling woman.

She turned and walked through the kitchen and out the back door.

"I'm just gonna go lock up behind her," Brad stammered.

"I might need to sleep with a light on tonight," Becky said. "Seeing how I'm alone and all. But, I'm closest to the attic at the moment. I'll head on up and bring back a box of wires and cables."

"You don't have to," Taryn said. "I think we're all pretty tired. We can dig for cables tomorrow."

"Word," Laurel said, shaking her head slightly. The voice had left her, its murmuring and whispering leaving a sense of fogginess behind. "It's only, what? Six-ish? Let's have some food and all hit the hay. Tomorrow's a free day with no scheduled activities, right?"

"Yep," Harmony said. "We have the parrot sanctuary tour on Friday."

"And manatees," Taryn said. "Some of us are going to swim with manatees."

"Perfect," Laurel said. "There'll be plenty of time to hang out together tomorrow. Let's eat something and get some sleep."

Chapter 5

While the women who'd come in that evening carted their luggage to rooms upstairs, Brad pretended to help Clara make hamburgers, tuna salad, and a vegetable tray. No one believed he was sick any longer, so no one cared that he carried a bowl of vegetable dip to the dining room before taking a seat at the head of the thick and polished table.

The ladies were more interested in getting their bags opened and a few things hung in closets to let wrinkles fall out. Dress shoes and sandals took up residence along the base of closet floors and bags of toiletries sat beside beds and nightstands, awaiting nightly routines.

In the turtle room, Harmony Ross stepped away from her open suitcase, only partially emptied on her bed, unaware that its rollers already marred the pale green quilt. "Imma go help Clara."

"Be down in a minute," Kandy told her, opening her laptop on the other swamp-colored bed.

"Tell Tucker Auntie Harm says 'hey'," Harmony cooed, as she ducked out of their room.

In the egret room at the back, right corner of the house, Laurel stood at the window overlooking a single banyan tree surrounded by a multitude of greens giving way to water beyond. She could see the cottage where Mrs. Powell's porch light burned with the intensity of a super nova, here at the beginning of nightfall.

"Anything pretty out there?" Jackie asked her.

Laurel snickered. "You're joking, right? This is Florida. It's gorgeous out there. But that Grace Poole caretaker chick has a porch light that could guide ships from the Texas side of the Gulf."

"Nice reference. You think she's guarding a crazy woman in the attic? A crazy woman who hordes boxes of cables and wires?"

Laurel laughed outright at that.

"Seriously, though, whoever heard of a caretaker for an Airbnb living on the property?" Jackie asked. "That's just weird."

"Maybe they've had damage to the house before?" Laurel suggested. "She seemed kinda hung up on the 'be careful with things' part of the speech."

"I guess," Jackie agreed. "And I felt like she was whispering stuff to me the whole time. Totally freaky."

"Thank you! I swore I heard a voice, too. Like someone was interrogating me."

"And what was the meaning of 'that is acceptable' for the number of people here?" Jackie asked.

"Right? I'm sure Marigold or Jen told the owner how many guests were staying. The place is listed as sleeping up to twenty-four people. Remember reading that? We liked thinking we'd have extra room to spread out if Sue got on anyone's nerves. Now what's this caretaker gonna do if our number wasn't acceptable? Were we gonna toss the kids out?"

"Or Brad," Jackie said. She lowered her voice dramatically in imitation of Penny, "unless this house cures him of his anger."

Laurel giggled. "You're gonna get me in trouble this week, aren't you? I thought you were gonna start something when you asked Taryn how old she was."

"Hey. Legitimate question. And legitimate enough that Nurse Ratched asked it, too. Or at least a version of it. Asked her if she was the nanny," Jackie laughed.

Laurel turned away from the window, missing the flutter of bright red that shifted among the tree trunks and up, up, up into the canopy.

"Let's join 'em downstairs for some food."

~ ~ ~

The landing on the second floor offered a few options to guests. Turning left gave either a doorway to the primary suite or access to a convoluted hallway, obviously built for the purpose of increasing the paths and privacy upstairs.

The guest could, of course, stand on the landing and gaze out a window, watching the trees, water, and caretaker's cottage. Turning right gave a long hallway down the right side of the house with a set of unevenly spaced bedroom doors and a couple additional hackneyed hallways between them.

Or, finally, the guest could reach up and pull down the attic ladder—which appeared to have been unused for a decade or two—revealing a set of steep wooden steps that required no small amount of dexterity to climb.

This is the option Becky Ellexen went for before joining the rest of the group for dinner.

"Three points of contact," Becky muttered to herself, as she grasped the sides of the structure and began her ascent. She considered for a moment how difficult it might be to get back down the steps with a box in hand.

Hopefully the box would be small.

Or the cables labeled.

She huffed at herself as she stepped onto the squeaky floorboard: "Not sturdy at all."

She wished she'd changed out of the cowboy boots into something less bulky, less likely to plunge through the plywood planks bathed in minimal light around her shadow from the window's dusk-light behind her. She squinted into the dark air to look for a dangling string that might indicate a light pull. So far, all she saw was floating dust in the beam from the single round window.

"Keys," she said out loud.

While her keychain had set off alarms going through security back in Dallas, she'd pulled it out of her carry-on at the Orlando Enterprise lot to attach the rental's key fob. She pulled the mass of keys, fob, mini-pepper spray, and pocket flashlight from her cargo pants and twisted the silver LED top.

The concentrated beam cut the air precisely. She moved it around the edges of the room, taking in the smallness of the space.

'Glad I didn't stand up fast,' she thought, shining the beam at the low rafter mere inches from her face.

Among the rafters closer to the outer wall, cobwebs strung between cotton candy-looking bags of spider nests and egg sacs, making her shudder. The tell-tale signs of rodent tooth marks and droppings lined the wood. One area looked damaged by water, possibly rotting, and she shone the light above it by instinct to assess the leaking area.

She couldn't see where rain ingressed, but as if her light had activated the green-and-black mold, the musty smell reached her then.

'If workers brought anything up here, they wouldn't go far with it to get the hell back outta Dodge,' she thought.

Moving the light to sweep the area closer to her feet, she saw a number of crates and boxes that had been nailed or taped shut for what looked like a couple dozen years. The nails were rusted under their layers of dust and most of the tape was yellowed to an almost brown where it had popped loose under the ages of attic heat.

Only a couple of boxes looked recently placed, so she moved cautiously, stooping under the near rafter, to assess those two.

With the mass of keys and mini flashlight in one hand, she only had her left hand to unfold the box flaps that had been tucked into one another. Grumbling at herself and the task, she muttered, "come on, come on," before the flaps gave way in a mini explosion of cardboard and attic dust. She coughed as she knelt beside the box and grabbed a handful of crinkled paper to pull out.

"Probably asbestos on everything," she muttered before sharply exclaiming, "Ow!"

She yanked back her hand and stuck her index finger in her mouth, sucking in the coppery taste of blood.

'*What the hell?*' she thought.

The light revealed a thick metal needle angled up from the crinkly paper.

"Great," she said, reaching more carefully around the needle-like pin. She tugged it out, pulling a bent hat pin from the mess of papers.

Its coloring was that of brushed nickel, but it didn't weigh enough to be anything but stainless steel. The round bauble at one end was ornately designed in a repeating pattern of curved plates to create a hollow ball. It would definitely work to hold a hat in place if a woman from the 1930s or '40s owned it.

'*A nice* something old *for Jen,*' she figured.

She set it on the floorboard to move the crinkly papers around, gently, cautiously, thinking, '*this is probably* not *the workers' box.*'

After a minute of finding merely antique jewelry and lots of paper, she shoved the box to the side and moved on her knees toward the other that had the least amount of dust. It flopped open much more easily and she smiled.

"That's more like it," she said aloud.

Extension cords and cables were snaked around in a mass of plastic spaghetti. There appeared to be no rhyme or reason to it, but at least she was on the right track now. Common sense had her reach for a white, thin cord.

Success.

She pulled the computer-related cable from the mess. She had to struggle a bit to yank it from under a black extension cord tangle, and finally held it up to the dark air where someone colorful and solid knelt beside her.

She gasped.

She gasped in putrid air that tasted of the mold behind this silent person. Before she could expel the breath with any sort of sound, the person's eyes and mouth opened wide with a squeaking, guttural groan.

Opened wide to expose red where the whites of his black eyes should have been. Opened wide to expose black where the pink of his tongue should have been. Opened wide to expose pointed teeth as if they'd each been sharpened by inaccurate blows of heavy, breaking stones.

The closeness of the sudden ugliness silenced any scream she could have sounded off. It stopped her breath in the top of her lungs where it held for a second—for a short, sharp, shocking second before the person lunged onto her.

The white, mini cable flopped down the steep staircase ladder and landed on the hardwood floor with an almost imperceptible flop.

A moment later, the steps began to rise, slowly, creaking, folding back up into the attic as if they'd not been disturbed for a decade or two.

Chapter 6

A few of the old friends stayed up late Wednesday night visiting in the parlor, letting Marigold in when her cab brought her to the manor. A few of the old friends went upstairs shortly after dinner to sleep off the stress of traveling to a destination wedding in Central Florida.

As they had anticipated, Thursday started off as a slow, easy day for the women who had come to Crystal River to see yet another college friend get married. Penny and her little brother woke up ready to remind anyone who would listen of the promise of "adult supervision" so they could jump in the pool.

Laurel shuffled her feet out of the egret room around nine, following the bracing aroma of coffee to the kitchen. There, she found Taryn had already joined Clara in setting out mugs and spoons for travel-weary friends to caffeinate.

"Aw, that's exactly what I need," Laurel told them.

"Good morning," Clara said, leaning against the closed dishwasher. "Did you sleep well?"

"Like a rock. Is there creamer?"

"Yep. Fridge."

"Look what I found on the landing this morning," Taryn said. "The gal in the cowboy boots—"

"Becky," Clara interjected.

"—must've grabbed it from the attic after all and then dropped it before she went to bed. I was so tired last night I didn't even notice it when I went up to bed, but this morning, there it was, bright as day. So-oh, we can give it a try on the TV and have everything available to us in an instant."

Laurel thought that sounded great but was intent on getting coffee into her soul before she talked about electronics and entertainment. The safety seal on the creamer offered too much resistance, but, once off, released an awful, sour stink from the white bottle.

"Ugh!"

"Oh my God," Clara said. "I can smell that clear over here."

Laurel clamped the lid down on the bottle and quickly shoved it in the freezer. "We can't drink that, can we?"

"What a waste," Taryn said. "That was a huge carton. What's the expiration date?"

Laurel ignored the question, not interested in bringing it back out of the freezer. Instead, she looked in the fridge for any other creamers. It appeared to be the only one, but something else had a strange odor. She poked around to find what was stinking while Clara reasoned what had gone wrong.

"I just bought it," Clara said. "We went to the store when we got here and brought everything right to the house. It shouldn't have gone bad in two days."

"It's okay," Laurel assured her. "We can always grab another creamer when we're out and about today, right? Is this the leftover tuna salad from last night?" She brought a Rubbermaid container out of the fridge and held it closer to her nose for a second. Foul. "Ugh. Oh no."

"What? Is it bad, too?" Clara asked.

"Did the fridge turn off overnight or something?" Taryn asked. She rose from the table and walked to the refrigerator alongside Clara. The three stared in, none brave enough to grab any more containers.

"Try the milk," Clara said.

"Nuh-uh," Laurel said. "I don't want to sniff that. Maybe the cottage cheese?"

"Check the expiration date first," Taryn suggested.

"What are you guys doing?" a sultry voice asked from the pass-through doorway.

"Good morning, Marigold!" Taryn almost shouted. She seemed overly excited to see her new friend. "We think the fridge is on the fritz. Maybe you could mention it to Mrs. Powell?"

"Mmm, yeah, I guess I need to go visit this caretaker woman this morning, don't I?"

"I could go with you if you want," Taryn offered.

"Maybe," Marigold said. She reached up to zhuzh her twists as she moved slowly, effortlessly into the kitchen. She carried herself with an easy grace, despite the yawn she tried to block with a well-manicured hand. "But I'm not ready to face that yet. I need some coffee. I have to go pick up some flowers this morning, too. Has Becky or Harmony come down yet?"

"Not yet," Clara said.

"I might need to use the van, then," Marigold spoke directly to Clara. "Do you have the keys, or can you get 'em from Brad for me?"

"What do you need the van for?" Brad asked, walking in on cue.

"Flowers."

"Flowers," he huffed. "You can't take the car the girls rented in Orlando?"

"They haven't come down yet," Clara said.

"And that's a reason to take the van?" he groused. "I need to run out and get something for my head. It's splitting. I'll be back with the van shortly."

Marigold frowned. "I can bring back headache medicine."

"I have Aleve," Taryn offered.

Laurel ignored it all. She and Jackie had guessed Brad's problem the first time they'd met him at Clara's wedding. That had been five years before, and the man wasn't exactly solving his addictions. If he wanted to leave the house to get whatever libation he needed this morning, no one could stop him.

Laurel picked up the container of vegetable dip from the night before while the argument over vehicles began behind her. She opened the container, turned, and held it out where its stench could have the greatest impact for stopping a fight.

"I think this has gone bad, too," she announced.

"Oh my God!" Brad said. "What's wrong with you? You're making me sick!"

"Laurel," Clara said.

~ ~ ~

"Yep, I think that's gone bad, too," Marigold agreed, turning on her heel to go back around the back side of the house to the staircase.

She didn't have patience for drama and needed to contact the flower shop about times and schedules. She almost bumped into Sue as she rounded the corner on the right side of the house.

"Good God, Sue, you startled me."

Sue was standing motionless in the middle of the hall, staring at one of five framed, black and white prints hanging in a perfect row. If not for the doorway to the washroom under the stairs breaking the pattern, they would have been perfectly spaced.

"Good morning," Sue said. "Sorry 'bout that. Just looking at the art. It's bugging me."

Marigold didn't want to get dragged into one of Sue's wacky conversations, but she felt it happening. "Mmm. I need to get my phone—"

"Do you think it's odd that these are pictures?" Sue asked.

Yep, the wacky conversation was happening. Marigold sighed and moved in to take a closer look at the prints.

The first one depicted a Native American woman in the foreground with a cluster of trees, some fallen and some standing, behind her. Next to her, the skeleton of a covered wagon held wooden barrels and stacks of folded blankets. Even though the print had been developed in black and white, one could tell everything had been full of color in reality. Everything from the woman's sash across her waist and breast to the blankets to the vegetation promised the real scene had been full of vibrance.

"The Native Americans believed that the tintype photographers were taking their souls when they took their pictures," Sue said, the myth rolling off her tongue as if it were the Gospel. "Why would these be pictures instead of drawings?"

Marigold didn't want to get pulled into an educational argument, so she didn't address the idea of what Native Americans did or didn't believe. Instead, she said, "there are tons of pictures in textbooks and museums. Maybe these are from a museum."

Sue turned her head to face Marigold. "Doesn't that seem a little disrespectful?"

"To hang pictures from a museum?"

"This is Seminole country. It's not respectful to flaunt their beliefs," Sue said.

"You'll have to take that up with Mrs. Powell. I have to call the flower shop."

"Don't you have an appointment with them?" Sue asked.

"I do, but Becky's not come down with the keys yet and Brad's going 'out' with the van in a minute. I don't want to keep paying an Uber to take me around the county. That was the point of having two vehicles, you know?"

Sue nodded and looked back at the picture of the woman. "Maybe I'll talk to Mrs. Powell about the pictures."

Chapter 7

By mid-afternoon, Mr. Brandon was seated by the pool in a sunny spot and the Brandon children were happily splashing away. Laurel and Jackie had chaise loungers in a shady spot while Clara had pulled her chair closer to the elderly gentleman in the sunshine. Taryn worked at setting up some Bluetooth speakers with her smartphone to provide music and Kandy helped Brad deliver beers to everyone who wanted one.

Harmony figured out which room was Becky's and went upstairs to bang on her door.

"You're missing all the fun," Harmony called through the door.

Marigold pulled the van into the gravel clearing at the front of the manor and walked through the house to the back lanai where the pool party was getting started.

"You guys look like you're parked for the night," she said.

Jackie grinned at her. "As it should be when one stays up too late drinking on a Wednesday."

"One spends Thursday staying up late drinking by the pool?" Marigold teased.

"Exactly," Jackie agreed. "Did you get the flowers delivered?"

"Mmm-hmm. Boutonniere and corsages are now in production. You may from now on refer to me as The Bridesmaid Who Gets Things Done."

"Are you going over to Mrs. Powell's now?" Taryn asked. "I don't mind going with you if you need someone to go along."

Jackie winked at Marigold but didn't say anything out loud.

"Sure, that'd be great," Marigold said. "Let me throw my purse in my room. I'll be right back down."

She made it about halfway up the stairs before she met Harmony.

"Hey. I can't get Becky out of her room."

"Still in bed?" Marigold asked. "Is she sick?"

"I don't know. She's not answering her door. It's not really her style to ignore us, you know?"

Marigold glanced back down the stairs to make sure no one had followed her, and then said lowly, "she might be avoiding the newest member of the Scooby Gang."

Harmony nodded slowly. "That'd make more sense if Becka'd spent any time with her last night."

"Really?"

"Really. We were all in the front room together for maybe half an hour before Creepy Annie Wilkes showed up and then Becka went back upstairs to bed. She didn't even join us for dinner."

"Creepy Annie Wilkes," Marigold chuckled. "Y'all are making me excited about meeting this lady in person."

"You know, in fact, Becka didn't stick around that whole half hour down there. She wanted to call home, so she was up here for a bit before the creep show showed up."

"Okay. So, no time to get annoyed enough to hide out from Taryn all day today. She may be really sick."

Harmony shrugged her shoulders.

"I'm headed up, obviously. I'll check on her, too. You look like you're headed out for the pool party."

Harmony grinned. She didn't need a second invitation to go hang out with her friends.

"Hey, which room did she pick?" Marigold asked.

"The wolf room, down the first hallway, behind Taryn's room."

"Got it."

The tangled hallways of the second floor were a testament to the bed-n-breakfast afterthought nature of the house. It had once been someone's large home on a sugar plantation. The refurbishments mentioned in the Airbnb advertisement didn't spell out that new walls and halls had been erected to force additional bedrooms into the place but looking at the layout made it obvious—the walls and halls had been erected to force additional bedrooms into the place. More money could be made off more guests.

It was logical.

It never occurred to any of the wedding guests that something beyond profit necessitated luring more visitors to the house.

Marigold navigated the narrow hall between the crow room Taryn had chosen and the turtle room that Kandy and Harmony were sharing to get to the wolf room along the outer wall of the house. She knocked on Becky's door and waited a polite minute before knocking again and speaking, "Becky? Are you awake?"

No one answered, of course, so Marigold got bold and tried the doorknob. It turned easily. She opened the door inward to the daylit room where the bed was undisturbed, and the open suitcase on the folding luggage stand had been left partially unpacked from the evening before.

"This is wrong."

Becky's cell phone lay next to her purse on the bed.

"Very wrong," Marigold muttered, turning on her heel to march quickly back to the group.

Chapter 8

"I don't think we need to call nine-one-one to tell them our friend didn't sleep in her bed last night," Brad said.

"First of all, she's not your friend, is she?" Jackie snapped. "No, she's not. So, you can keep your opinion—"

"Okay," Laurel interrupted when she saw Clara's eyes growing wide. "Let's stay productive."

As Brad flipped them off—with both hands—and stomped toward the kitchen door, Laurel continued, "There's got to be a number for the local sheriff's office. Taryn, is that what you're looking up?"

"I mean, I could do that, sure. I was, um, looking up places around here that Becky could have walked to in a reasonable time."

"Why, again, are we thinking she went for a walk, after dark, in a swamp, without her phone?" Marigold asked.

Laurel held a hand out toward Marigold as if suggesting she lower her voice. "Harmony and Kandy are hitting the spots within quick driving distance, so let's focus on getting the authorities to help us. Taryn, could you—"

Clara had her phone to her ear by then and began speaking: "Yes, I need to report a missing person."

"There," Laurel said. "Productive."

Brad returned to the poolside with a beer open in one hand and the other five hanging from their plastic rings. He plopped down on his lawn chair and watched his wife talking to the police as if he would burn holes through her with his glare.

The women listened, watching him drink beer, and waiting for a miracle. Clara's side of the conversation didn't bode well for finding Becky that day. At one point, Clara signaled to Laurel and moved the phone to ask, "what was Becky wearing last night? Cargo pants? Didn't she have on tan cargo pants?"

Laurel nodded, wishing she could impart some calming influence on her friend. Clara's reddened face and short, fast breaths pointed to a stress level akin to reliving trauma. How many times had this poor woman fought to maintain a calm voice while answering questions from a police dispatcher?

By the time she pressed the red "end" button, Clara looked dejected.

"Have the authorities here on speed dial, do you?" Brad asked.

"What did they say?" Laurel asked.

"We have another twenty-four hours before Becky will be considered missing. Right now, she could be considered just away from the house or something. It's very confusing, but because she's an adult, you know, on vacation..."

As her thought trailed away, Brad crushed the empty beer can and let it fall to the ground. It bounced on the paving stones.

"That's real nice," Jackie said.

"Did they suggest anything for us to do?" Laurel asked. "What should we be doing?"

"Leave all outdoor lights on tonight," Clara said, almost absently.

"That's it?" Laurel asked.

"We can post on social media that we're looking for her, if we think she would be okay with people knowing she's not at home. And if we know the places she likes to hang out, we can check those. But..." Again, Clara let her thought trail away.

The women understood her despondence. What places in Central Florida were the same as Dallas? And why would Becky go to those if she was on vacation?

Heavy footsteps came from the kitchen then and the group looked at Sue appearing in the doorway. Her ample form took up quite a bit of the space when she held out her arms as she did then. "My friends," she said. "I can feel Becky is near us."

Brad snorted with derision. "This oughta be good."

Jackie put her hand to her face and pinched the bridge of her nose.

"She is near the house and her spirit is afraid. Lost. Confused. We need to seek her out and bring her back."

"That sounds about stupid," Brad said.

Sue leveled him with her gaze, perfectly serious. "We mock what we don't understand."

"I'll help you seek her out," Taryn said. "Do we need to walk around the perimeter of the house?"

Laurel gave Taryn a kind smile. She thought it was sweet of her to humor Sue at such a time.

"It would please Becky's spirit greatly to see such cooperation," Sue answered. "But, I think, I can help her spirit find its way back if I am unhindered."

"I'm gonna see if Mrs. Powell can help us," Marigold said. "I need to see her about our contract anyway, right?"

Jackie made a scoffing sound. "Countess Bathory prob'ly has her."

Kandy frowned. "That's horrible."

Jackie shrugged. "Easier to believe than this idea she walked off into the swamp."

Brad chortled. "You're suggesting the caretaker kidnapped a healthy forty-year-old woman and is hiding her in a cottage."

"I don't actually believe it," Jackie said. "I'm just saying it's *easier* to believe of that creeptastic lady than believing Becky wandered away—"

"Okay. Then maybe one of us kidnapped her," Brad snarked. "Is that easier to believe? You think I took her somewhere and left her?"

Clara gasped. "Bradley!"

Laurel couldn't believe what she was hearing at that point. While her girlfriend antagonized Brad into practically admitting he'd harmed their friend, Laurel tossed frightening scenario after frightening scenario in her mind. She believed Brad was a wife-beating cretin and capable of doing harm to any one of them if left alone with any one of them, but she didn't believe he would be so brash as to follow through on kidnapping—or worse. She climbed off the chaise lounge and walked over to Marigold, who still held her purse and a look of despair.

"This is getting out of hand," Laurel said. "Do you want to go over to the cottage together?"

Marigold nodded, as if she were unable to form words at this point.

~ ~ ~

Susan Stein hadn't always believed in ghosts and talking to the spirit world, but upon entering college, she'd encountered enough paranormal activity to give the concepts a try. Taking on Tarot reading gave her some extra income for textbooks and guided her deeper into her spirituality. Now, at age forty-two, Sue had confidence in herself and in her ability to sense the supernatural.

At the Manatee Moss Hidden Manor, something supernatural not only hung around, it was filled with anger and worry. Something wanted its home to be respected and cared for properly. Sue believed she could feel a vibration, an energy welcoming her into the manor, but that same energy hesitated to extend a hand of friendship. Bringing guests to the house put the property in danger of disrespect and damage, thus the spirit guarding the estate was on edge.

Or so she felt.

Sue wasn't sure if Taryn understood spirituality and being kind to the supernatural world, but it was sweet of the young lady to offer to accompany her out here in search of Becky's spirit. But Sue was honest in telling Taryn she didn't want to be hindered. Whatever guarded this place had enough animosity to become dangerous if it felt dishonored. Sue wanted to remain open and positive, and she didn't need anyone's negativity or disbelief polluting the process.

By the time she reached this thought, Sue was far enough into the swamp that she couldn't see the beige house any longer. She knew exactly where it was. One didn't wander into a dense forest of trees and bramble without one's GPS on one's cell phone monitoring north and south, etcetera. She had a clear signal, almost full charge, and could see her path clearly on the phone's screen.

She put the phone in her tunic pocket and spread her arms open wide to inhale the fragrance of the moss and greenery around her. She closed her eyes so her other senses would sharpen.

Within a few seconds, she could sense a change in the environment. Something in the breeze carried a scent that wasn't altogether natural. Not altogether friendly.

Without opening her eyes, without lowering her arms, she turned to her right, her soft-cushioned loafers squishing on the swamp floor. Her hand brushed something soft among the tree limbs as she turned. For some reason, that bothered her enough for her to open her eyes.

A mouse-sized spider with long, strong legs supporting its body couldn't get away from her as she turned into its web. Her wrist arrested its scramble toward the safety of trees.

She flinched.

It bit her.

The fangs were surprisingly pointed and broke her skin easily, sinking into the meat of her forearm.

With a yelp, she snatched her arms toward her torso and the eight-legged beast, frightened as well, came along for the ride. She yelped again as it bit again.

She waved her arm, flinging the spider away as she jumped backward. Her foot slipped on a mossy rock, releasing more of the aroma that had, moments before, been so pleasant, so integral to the atmosphere, so much a part of her process.

She fell and rolled and crashed through bramble and brush, hitting her head against first a stump and then a rock as she tumbled down an incline toward puddles of swamp water.

She splashed there and came to rest, her chest heaving. Incredible pain. Broken bones. Labored breathing.

She needed help.

She fumbled with slow, bleeding fingers to find the pocket in her tunic, and to find it empty. Looking up the long, slimy incline, she wondered where along the drop she could find her phone. And *how* she could find it with darkness tunneling her vision to a mere pinpoint of light blinking out.

Chapter 9

Laurel guided Marigold toward a stone path off the back of the lanai, holding a gate open for her. It clicked closed behind them and they made their way toward the cottage with its beckoning porch light.

The closer they moved toward the little house, the more Laurel thought it looked like a shed than a cottage. It had the tell-tale front porch with Adirondack rocking chair next to the painted front door, but there was no feeling of cuteness to the house itself. No stonework. No chimney. No lacy curtains on the single window beside the front door. No flowerpots to denote an elderly woman with a green thumb might be inside. It looked lonely and cold instead of cottagelike and comfy.

"This looks stark," Marigold said quietly.

"Agreed," Laurel said.

"So, the lady's creepy?"

"Yeah. She gave this kinda harsh vibe, like she didn't want us renting this place after all. Told us how to keep the kitchen clean. That sort of thing."

"Great. I hope she has some ideas for finding Becky. There's gotta be a place on the property where Becky would go, right?"

Laurel didn't have that confidence but wanted to. "We'll ask."

As they approached the little house, they could hear Mrs. Powell moaning inside. The front window was open, its glass raised and no screen stopping the swamp's mosquitoes from getting in or the sound of distress from getting out. The women exchanged a look of concern and stepped up the pace, achieving the porch more quickly.

Laurel was reaching to knock on the door when Marigold grabbed her arm and pulled her away. The look on her face was difficult to read. A mix of horror, disgust, and amusement danced in Marigold's dark features.

She put her hand over her mouth as if to keep herself from saying something, but Laurel could see a light of mischievousness flickering in her brown eyes. Something was not as dire as the moaning would suggest. Marigold tilted her head toward the window to indicate Laurel should look in.

Laurel instantly regretted it.

Mrs. Powell lay naked on her bed, lazily writhing as if in the throes of slow passion. Laurel felt her own face contort into a mask of disgusted confusion as Mrs. Powell's contorted with something that might have been ecstasy.

Laurel tilted her head to the side, trying to understand why this looked so wrong. Why was the old woman deriving any pleasure from wiggling around when her hands were in the air?

"Oh my God," Laurel breathed.

Something she couldn't see flattened Mrs. Powell's wrinkled breasts and pressed her open legs with invisible pressure onto the quilt where she lay.

The woman wasn't alone.

As if the crone suddenly realized she was observed, she snapped her head to the side and fixed her eyes on the open window. Both Marigold and Laurel flung themselves to the wooden porch floor as Mrs. Powell moved her head. Unsure if they'd dove away in time or not, they heard a shriek of unholy sound and the creak of the bedframe.

"Go!" Marigold mouthed, pushing Laurel toward the shrubbery and bramble to the right of the cottage.

They ducked into the undergrowth and stickers, coming to an abrupt halt to keep it all from shaking before the front door flew open. Mrs. Powell appeared on the front porch wearing a long, bland robe and holding a double barrel shotgun. Her dark eyes scoured the landscape before her, searching, seeking out whatever had been at her window.

Laurel realized she was squeezing Marigold's hands. The two fought to control their breathing, trying to be the quietest part of the swamp around them.

From the other side of the area that passed for a yard in front of the cottage, a blue heron lifted off, drawing Mrs. Powell's attention. The ancient woman moved with the speed of a striking scorpion. She raised the shotgun to her shoulder, sighted the bird, and squeezed the trigger, all in a fast, fluid, loud motion. The bird squawked once and fell to the ground in an explosion of blue-gray feathers.

Laurel choked back the gasp in her throat. Marigold merely closed her eyes, tight, squinting them against reality. They could hear their friends reacting at the pool not far from them, shouts of swearing, chairs scooting across the stone pavers as people jumped up.

Mrs. Powell lowered the gun and walked back into her house, slamming the door. They heard the click of the deadbolt sliding into place and took off for the pool.

"I'm telling you that was a gunshot," Brad was shouting.

"And I'm telling you no one would shoot a gun in the middle of a residential area," Jackie responded.

"Does this look residential to you?" Brad asked, waving his arm in a wide, sweeping gesture.

"Guys, guys, you're not gonna believe this," Marigold panted as she and Laurel ran up to the screen surrounding the pool.

~ ~ ~

In their room that night, Jackie sat on the end of the bed and watched Laurel setting her clothes out for the next day.

"I'm surprised at some of the things you did today," Jackie finally said.

"You mean helping Sue?"

"That, yeah, but the whole day was just weird. And you acted like nothing was wrong. Don't you think Sue should have come running when that shotgun went off? Don't you think it's crazy that Marigold thinks there's a ghost in the cottage with Mrs. Powell? And do you not see how manipulative and horrible Brad is?"

Laurel didn't think it was necessary to defend Marigold's belief in a ghost. She'd seen it, too. Or, to be more precise, she'd seen the evidence of it. But she didn't want to argue every point Jackie was making. She went for the easy one. "Of course, I see how crazy Brad is."

"Don't you think we should help Clara?" Jackie asked.

"What do you mean? Help her? *Instead* of helping Sue?"

"Maybe. I don't know. I just think it's strange that you side with Brad on everything."

Laurel thought about that for a second before responding. "First, I don't side with Brad. On anything. I want to diffuse what's going on there. Irritating him is only making things worse for Clara."

Jackie huffed. "Do you believe that?"

"Of course. Look, if we make him mad, he's going to take that anger out on her and the kids. Do you want to be responsible for the next bruise you see on her?"

"I can't believe I'm hearing this. We need to get her away from him, not coddle him into not beating her for a day."

"You're advocating breaking up her family by, what? Pissing off her husband bad enough while they're on a five-day vacation? Because I think they'll make it through this vacation still married, go home still married, and he'll continue beating her, still married. I think the more productive thing to do is get her some contact information for good counselors in her hometown."

Jackie shook her head. "Maybe. You have good experiences with family counselors, do you?"

Laurel shot her a look of "*we don't go there.*"

"But tomorrow, when we go on this group excursion, could you at least try to back *me* instead of him?" Jackie asked.

"Whoa. You know I always back you."

"Not really. Every comment you make is to get me to shut up."

Laurel sat down on the bed beside Jackie and placed a hand on her arm. "I hope you don't see things that way. I would never tell you to shut up. I will always back you. Okay?"

"Okay. And I suppose I always *stitch* you up. You got pretty scratched up in that hedgerow today."

Laurel sighed. "Yeah, it's gonna suck getting in saltwater tomorrow. Do you think any of these scratches could get infected? They're not all that deep, are they?"

Jackie frowned a bit. "I don't think they're so much deep as they are already-infected. You need some Bactine or something to seal 'em *before* you get in the water."

A commotion in the room next door interrupted them.

Chapter 10

When Taryn returned to her room, she put in her earbuds and set up her tablet to skype with her boyfriend back home. It took a few tries to get the cyber connection to work, and she blamed that on the Wi-Fi wackiness of the swamp. Soon, though, she had a full-screen picture of Kevin, a twenty-three-year-old brunette with puppy-dog eyes.

"Aw, it's great to see you," she said.

"Back atcha, Babe. How's Florida?"

She had already decided not to tell him the caretaker on the property was shooting animals. It would only make him worry.

"I mean, it's warm and muggy but it's November so it's not so bad, right? We all got in the pool here on the property this afternoon. Well, not *all* of us got in the water. Tomorrow I think a bunch of us get in the water with manatees. We have a group excursion that Jen and Jeremy arranged for their out-of-town guests. What are you doing?"

"Just polishing my sign for the contest."

"Oh. Great. Can I see?"

"Nope. Ya gotta wait like everybody else, Babe."

"You're such a tease. How are you feeling about the competition?"

"I'm not thinking about the competition," he said. "Only about my skills. I've just about got the 900-degree aerial so mastered that I can do it with my eyes closed."

"Kev, that's ahh-mazing."

"Yep." He looked into the web camera then. "I think I'm gonna do a couple easy nollies, maybe an inward heel flip, just to work my way up to the ramps, you know? And then, pow, when everyone's getting bored, pow, hit the big trick and score all the points."

"You've got this," she said.

"True dat. Hey, who you sharing a room with?"

"No one. A bunch of us girls share one of the bathrooms upstairs here, but I get my own room this trip."

"Then who's the guy?"

Taryn yanked her earbuds out as she spun off the back of the bed, ready to scream at Brad Brandon for invading her privacy. Her feet hit with loud, solid, thud-thuds that shook the old floorboards. And yet, she saw no one in her room.

There was no guy.

Turning back to the tablet, she didn't even laugh at Kevin's poor humor. "That's so not funny, Kev. One of the girls is totally missing, so we're all on edge."

"The dude was *just* there. And how does someone go missing?"

She missed his assertion because she was retrieving her earbuds, but she heard the tail end of his question.

"The gal named Becky from Dallas. She came in from the Orlando airport, so I didn't really get to know her, but last night she went up to her room and never came back down. When a couple of us checked on her today, she wasn't in her room. We think she went out for a walk before she went to bed last night and must've gotten turned around in the swamp or something. Kinda freaky, right?"

Kevin stared into the web camera for a few seconds and finally said, "I think you should come home. Get outta that freaky house."

Now she laughed. "So-oh, you're freaking out when you don't need to be."

"Seriously, Taryn. You should hop the next flight outta that clap-trap and come home."

"Because someone got lost in the swamp?"

"Because it doesn't feel right."

"You're starting to sound like this gal Sue, who, by the way, traveled with Becky from Orlando. I think Sue is from Illinois, but they met up in Orlando to drive over. The point is Sue is a little on the mystical side, if you know what I mean, and she thinks Becky's spirit is hanging out in the swamp outside. She's walking around the house and gardens to call Becky back, so, you know, she's really nice, but kinda wacky. She thinks Becky's spirit is hung up on something somewhere."

"Babe, seriously, stop talking. I don't know what this Sue lady is smoking, but you need to come home."

"I'll be home Monday morning. And you can show me your trophy."

"Or you can leave that freak joint now and be here to watch me win this trophy."

"You're not giving this place its props, Kev. Hang on. Someone's at the door."

She pulled out the earbuds again so she could untether herself and get to the door. Because she dropped the earbuds to the bed, she didn't hear him continue to bash the Manatee Moss Hidden Manor establishment. Because she hopped off the bed, she didn't see a shadow descend and minimize to a pinpoint that seemed to enter one of the earbuds, as if to travel into and through it. Because she skipped across the short space to the door, she didn't see a cloud of black consume the screen, engulfing the image of Kevin.

She didn't see him thrash against a corporeal darkness in his room a thousand miles away. She didn't hear him shriek and scream and finally gurgle against some angered presence crushing his windpipe, crushing his chest, and crushing his body down to the floor.

Laurel greeted Taryn at the door here in reality. "Hey. Are you all right in here?"

"Yeah, I'm just skyping with Kevin."

"Okay. We thought we heard you fall or something."

"Omigosh, that's so sweet of you to check on me. No, I just jumped off the bed. It's a long story. But everything's fine. Thank you for checking."

"No problem. Have a good night."

"You too!"

Taryn closed the door on Laurel's kind concern and walked back to the bed. There, the dark computer screen indicated Kevin had signed off. She frowned. "Well, good night to you, too, Babe." Closing the laptop, she reasoned out loud, "he needs his rest."

Chapter 11

Morning in the kitchen was more subdued than they wanted it to be. The friends wanted to be excited about the group excursion planned for them that day, but the shadow of Becky's disappearance hung over them. As each woman came in for breakfast or coffee, greeting one another with empathy, they tried to inject the day with some optimism.

Clara had taken a seat at the tiny table this morning instead of puttering around the kitchen cleaning up and pretending to be at home. Her kids were ready to go to their respective activities. The idea of swimming with manatees had Penny beyond hyper and practically jumping off the front porch, which is where she currently vibrated with energy. Patrick had been informed he'd be going on the other group excursion to see birds with his grandfather, and he was just as excited.

Brad walked into the kitchen still in boxers and a t-shirt and grumbled something at his wife.

"There's something I didn't need to see," Jackie muttered.

Laurel gave her a look that begged her to be kind.

From the dining room, Marigold called in: "Did you guys know the van is here for the manatee tour?"

"That's what I was gonna tell you guys," Brad said. "I put Penny in already."

"It's early?" Kandy asked.

Brad shrugged.

"We should get going, then," Clara suggested, rising from the table. She moved carefully, still babying the pain in her lower back.

Taryn swallowed a gulp of coffee and put her mug in the dishwasher. "So-oh, someone left a toothbrush in the washroom down here. Whoever's missing a toothbrush, that's where it is."

Clara handed a bagel to Brad. "For you."

"Is the cream cheese bad?" he asked, as if he expected to be poisoned.

"Jesus, Mary, and Joseph, no. I bought all new dairy yesterday. Everything's fine."

"Just making sure you're not handing me something to make me sick."

"Because that's what wives do," Kandy muttered, setting her mug next to the sink.

"Do you want to take this coffee with you?" Taryn asked her. "I mean, why waste a whole mug, right? I can put it in one of these travel cups for you if you want."

Kandy tightened her smile and said, "That would be great. Thank you."

Harmony peeked in from the pass-through. "Hey, guys, I'm gonna stay here today in case Becky tries to reach us."

Kandy walked over to discuss that with her while Taryn asked everyone in the room, "and whose mug is this one?"

"For the love of God," Jackie said under her breath.

"Oh, that's mine," Laurel said. "I'm done with it. I don't want to take it with me."

"I'll just put it in the dishwasher before we head out," Taryn said.

"Hey, what's taking you guys a year?" Brad asked. "Don't you have an appointment with this place? The van's here. The driver's waiting."

Jackie took Laurel's arm and practically dragged her from the doorway toward the front of the house.

"That's what I'm talkin' about," Brad said. "Everyone, let's move, move, move. My kid's gonna die in the back of the van and I'll get arrested for it because you people can't move out in the morning."

"I thought Sue was joining us for the manatee tour," Clara said. "I've not seen her come down yet."

"I haven't seen her since yesterday," Marigold said.

"Maybe she changed her mind and decided to do the bird tour with Kandy and them?" Taryn said.

"Great," Brad said. "I'm stuck with an old man, a three-year-old, and the chick who thinks she's clairvoyant."

"You'll have a great time with the birds, dear," Clara said, making her escape through the dining room.

When Marigold climbed into the van, she plopped onto the bench seat next to Clara and spoke lowly enough that Penny couldn't hear her worrying question. "You don't supposed Sue got lost out there, do you?"

Clara had pasted a smile on her face that didn't slip as she said, "I'm trying not to think about it."

"Wait," Laurel said. She leaned toward the two. "You don't suppose..."

Jackie pulled out her cell and brought up Sue's name. She pressed the button to call and waited, waited, waited while it rang and connected, and the call went to voice mail. She listened, waiting for the beep, and then said, "Sue, we're all going to freak out if you don't call back."

Laurel called Harmony. "Hey."

"What's up?" Harmony's voice asked. "You guys are still in the driveway."

"Yeah, would you check Sue's room? And see if she has her phone with her?"

There was a beat of silence before Harmony said, "you're kidding, right?"

"Check for me, please?"

"I'll call ya back."

Penny looked at Laurel seated next to her and asked, with childlike naivety, "do you suppose anyone else will go walking around alone?"

Laurel tried to laugh to set the child at ease. "We should use the buddy system, shouldn't we?"

"We do that at school. Everyone has a buddy when we line up."

"That's smart," Laurel said.

"I don't think I like the buddy at the house."

The hairs on the back of Laurel's neck stood on end. "You mean Patrick? I think he's a good buddy."

Penny shook her head and then lowered her voice to a sort of conspiratorial tone. "I mean the man with the ugly eyes. The one who needs more replacement souls."

Laurel's cell phone rang in her lap, causing her to jump.

"Christ," she muttered. Harmony's name appeared on her screen.

"Hey. Is Sue—"

"She's not in her room," Harmony said.

Her voice was not calm.

Chapter 12

With two of their friends missing, the group made a decision to alter the day's plans. They'd piled out of the van and were discussing the situation with Brad and Harmony while the driver waited patiently.

"I don't want to ruin Jen's wedding with talk of missing persons, okay?" Marigold said. "But we can't pretend this isn't crazy. I say we split up a little better. Clara, d'you wanna go ahead and keep Penny occupied with the manatee adventure thing? Taryn, can you do that, too? If you think about it, that's a huge van about to pull up to the planned group activity with a whole lot of the group not there. Jen's gonna notice that."

Taryn jumped back in the van to sit next to Penny, signaling she was ready to go along with the plan.

"I'll go nuts if I stay around here," Jackie said. "I can't handle this kind of stress. I'll go on the adventure thing and pretend we're all happy happy joy joy here." She looked at Laurel. "What you wanna do?"

"I think I want to stay here and help find Sue. She couldn't have gone far if she was only walking around the house and garden, right?"

Jackie nodded. "Promise me something."

"Yeah?"

"You don't go anywhere alone."

Laurel put her arms around Jackie in a comforting embrace they both needed and whispered against her soft blonde bob, "I promise."

Brad slapped the side of the van, startling all of them. "Sounds like you gals have made a decision to ruin your vacation plans. Good for you. I'm taking Patrick to the parrot place. If you three are staying here, I'm leaving my dad with you."

"Wait, what?" Clara said. "We looked over the Ziggy's Haven website together and you said your dad would love—"

"I'm not babysitting that old fart *and* a kid," Brad snapped. "One or the other. Or would you rather switch places and *you* can babysit them?"

Jackie turned an absolute glare on the man, waiting for the ultimatum to play out.

"Brad," Clara sighed. "Your father—"

"Is a pain in the ass," Brad finished. He slapped the side of the van again and shouted up to the driver, "I think you're ready to go!"

He stepped back from the van, waving a sort of sarcastic salute to his wife as he turned toward the house.

"Why couldn't *he* have gone missing?" Marigold whispered to Laurel.

Laurel shushed her, as if anyone was listening to them.

"Seriously," Marigold said lowly. "We need to convince that moron to wander into the swamp and 'not return.'"

"That sounds a little premeditated to me," Laurel told her. "Let's just send him off to this bird sanctuary and make a plan for finding the girls."

Chapter 13

When the two sets of wedding guests returned to the house that evening, Laurel ordered pizzas to be delivered for their exhausted, combined group. Brad had bought more alcohol and proceeded to fill the only tub in the house with ice and cans of beer as if they had something to celebrate. As he moved toward the front door to collect more bags of ice, Jackie confronted him from the dining room.

"Do you think we should be hosting a frat party when the police are coming over?" Jackie asked him.

"Your girlfriend is the one ordering pizzas," he snarked.

"For food," Jackie said.

"And what makes you think police are gonna give you bitches the time of day?"

"It's been another twenty-four hours," Clara said.

"If anyone in this house calls the police, I'll have them arrest you for harassment," Brad said. "It's stupid to think—"

"Don't you have more ice to bring in?" Jackie asked him. "Clara, what's the number for the cops? I'll call so this jackass has me to deal with and no one else."

Brad and Jackie stared at one another, glaring until Brad snarled a smile. "You think you're pretty tough, don't you?" he asked.

"I *am* pretty tough," she answered. "Clara, the number?"

Brad held up both hands to flip her off, showcasing a significant bandage on his right index finger.

"What did you do to your hand?" Clara asked.

"One of those damn birds bit me. We need to sue that Zippity Do Dah place."

Kandy walked through the foyer toward the parlor then, absently responding, "can't sue them when they told you to keep your fingers out of the cages."

Harmony signaled to Laurel from the kitchen, motioning her to step away from the group in the dining room area. "There's something strange upstairs," Harmony whispered.

"There's something strange everywhere," Laurel murmured. "What's up?"

"Um, well, when I went up just now, um...your room...as I walked by your room...it stinks."

Laurel frowned. "What do you mean?"

"Like...horrible stink. Like when a mouse dies-in-your-wall stink."

Laurel could see Harmony was fighting back tears. The implication in what she said wasn't lost on Laurel. She looked back to see Clara and Jackie huddled over a cell phone. Brad had gone back out to get more of his party supplies.

Ever the level-headed one, Laurel said, "Okay, let's go up and see what's going on before we alarm anyone, right?"

Harmony nodded.

They took the back passthrough so as not to disturb anyone, as if being sneaky. As they walked toward the front of the house to climb the staircase, Laurel noticed each of the five framed prints on the hallway wall were tilted, no longer perfect. 'Disrespectful,' she thought. 'Shouldn't be disrespectful.'

In the front room, Taryn hooked up her tablet to the smart TV to show pictures from the day to Patrick and Mr. Brandon, which Laurel thought was an excellent distraction for all of them. But as she and Harmony approached her room at the top of the stairs, she could smell the faint whiff of rotting fruit. Something was off. She opened the door to her room and the stench deepened. Rotten fruit and a touch of feces permeated the air. She and Harmony exchanged frightened glances before they both looked up at the ceiling.

"Oh my God, she went up to the attic Wednesday night," Laurel said.

"But she brought that cable down," Harmony said. "We found..."

Laurel turned and went to the landing where the attic access sat closed and quiet. "It looks like no one's been up there in years," she muttered, reaching for the hanging latch.

When she pulled it down, the rickety steps lowered, and a powerful stink of death puffed outward like a storm cloud. She choked and gagged.

"Oh no, oh no, oh no," Harmony began moaning.

"Go get help," Laurel said.

"Oh no, oh no, oh no." Harmony dropped to her knees on the landing, holding her sides and rocking gently. "This isn't real. It's not real."

She recognized Harmony went into shock, so Laurel pulled herself together. Growing up in Detroit gave one a set of coping skills that kicked in like instinct when others around you start to fall apart. "Okay, stay here. Don't move. I'll be right back."

As she hurried down the steps, she heard Penny asking, "Oh, gross Patrick, did you fart? It stinks!"

The whole house would soon smell of death. As she stepped into the foyer at the base of the steps, she came face to face with Brad. Two bags of ice filled his arms and he looked none too pleased to be presented with her as an obstacle.

"You're in my way," he complained.

"Help," she said simply.

~ ~ ~

On the landing, Harmony fought to keep from vomiting. The smell had been strongest when Laurel had first opened the attic access door, but it still wafted down the ladder-like steps and still surrounded her like a cloud she couldn't deny any longer. Her friend was probably dead up there. She had to check. She owed it to Becky to be sure.

With shaking hands, she reached for the steps and began to climb.

~ ~ ~

Brad stared at Laurel's wide eyes and said, "are you screwing around? Because this ice is freezing cold, and I don't want to stand here—"

"No, really, I think we found Becky, and," she gulped and glanced to her left to make sure the kids in the parlor weren't paying attention to them. They were happily distracted by fart jokes. "And I think it's terrible."

Something in her demeanor must have struck a chord with him. He sort of tossed-and-dropped the ice bags to the side of the foyer. The sudden, banging ruckus startled everyone to attention. One of the bags broke, scattering ice across the entryway to the dining room, causing Jackie and Clara to curse.

"Nothing to see here," he lied, following Laurel back up the stairs.

She inwardly chastised herself for asking Brad for help, but he was the first person she'd run into. And he was an adult male. Shouldn't a man be able to climb into the attic and assess the welfare of a woman?

As they approached the landing, she shuddered at both the odor and the fact that Harmony was gone.

"Up there," Laurel said, pointing at the attic space.

"Yeah, I figured," Brad said. "So that stink is your dead friend?"

"God, Brad, can you show some compassion?" she asked. "Harmony noticed the smell and it's definitely coming from the attic."

"So, you want me to climb up there to do what? Smell it better?"

"Could you just check to see—"

"Is everything okay up there?" Jackie called up.

Laurel closed her eyes against reality crashing in. "Brad, please."

"Yeah, fine, I'll be the hero for you."

He grabbed the side of the steps as Harmony let out a shriek above them.

"Holy shit!" Brad shouted.

~ ~ ~

When Harmony stood up in the attic, she came face to face with the same rafter Becky had been next to Wednesday night. She wasn't quite as tall as Becky had been because she walked barefoot tonight. The rafter still startled her with its closeness, but that wasn't what made her scream for help.

She could see the clump of keys in a patch of light and moved to pick them up.

"Oh, Becka. Why'd you come up here alone?"

It didn't occur to her that she asked the question out loud while alone herself.

Harmony took a slow step out of the patch of light, stooping under the low rafters, toward the strengthening smell. She held one hand up to her nose as if blocking the particles responsible for the offense. As she lowered her left foot down, she was moving forward. Her body weight, leaning over to avoid hitting her head on low, spider-heavy rafters, gave her no chance to stop the momentum as her foot came down on something sharp.

Something pointy drove upward as she tried to turn and twist off of it. A stainless-steel pin poked through the top of her foot, surprising her with metal, blood, and pain.

Chapter 14

Jackie didn't need more than that to come barreling up the stairs. Laurel could hear other commotion going on below, but she was more interested in helping her friend than in finding out who was charging to the rescue. Brad had taken a step back.

It took several minutes to drag Harmony down to the bathroom where Marigold and Laurel iced her foot before yanking the hat pin back out. Her shriek rent all their nerves. And it preceded a serious banging on the front door.

"That'll be the cops," Jackie muttered.

"Thank God," Laurel said.

Interestingly enough, Brad went to answer the door. Luckily enough, the cops had heard Harmony shriek and didn't believe Brad when he said everything was "all right" at the manor.

While one of the officers called for backup, another asked where the scream had come from.

"One of the girls hurt her foot. That's all. She's upstairs in the bathroom."

The officer immediately headed up the stairs.

Penny turned to Taryn and said, "My dad usually has to go visit friends when the police come over. I wonder if he'll go visit friends here."

Taryn wasn't sure how to respond to that, so she re-focused Penny's attention on the manatees in the pictures. "Where did your brother go? I thought he was excited about seeing the manatee pictures."

"The man with the ugly eyes took him to the lanai."

"What man?"

"The old man who lives here." Penny pointed to the hallway. "His picture's on the wall. He has ugly eyes, so I don't like to look at him. But Patrick doesn't see how ugly he is."

Taryn frowned at this. "Nobody lives here anymore. This is a rental house now. Why do you think someone lives here?"

Penny shrugged and pointed at one of the sea mammals on the screen—one that was swimming away from the camera. "I think this manatee is afraid of the man."

Taryn looked where the child was pointing and squinted at the shadows cast by the snorkelers from the day's excursion. Things were starting to get a little weird in the parlor. "Penny, stay here for me, okay?"

The child nodded.

Taryn scurried toward the dining room where Clara and Kandy were cleaning up the ice mess and answering questions from the officer who had arrived. As she hurried in, her foot landed on an ice cube and she slid into the officer. He caught her, but the craziness of it made her giggle.

She felt silly. The crazy idea she was coming to share with them suddenly felt ridiculous as well. She giggled more.

"Oh em gee, you guys," she laughed. "I'm losing my mind."

"Are the kids still with you?" Clara asked.

"Mm, Penny just told me Patrick went out back." She giggled some more. "She said a man with ugly eyes took him outside."

"A man?" the officer asked. "What man?"

"I mean, the only guys here are his dad and his grandpa, so–oh, it's all good."

"Out back?" Clara repeated. "Patrick went out back? But Brad is upstairs, isn't he?"

Taryn felt herself sliding further into silliness. "I don't know. I saw him right here a minute ago."

Clara's face turned ashen as her mother's intuition slammed her in the gut. "The pool," she whispered.

"Take me to the pool," the officer demanded.

For the second time that night, a woman's shriek filled the air when Clara found her young son floating lifelessly atop the water, his body askew in deep blue with its clothing billowed around him. His mop of unruly hair now swirled like cotton candy masses around his head.

This time, a woman's shriek rent their nerves with its hysteria.

This time, the cry was more than mere pain.

This time, the scream was followed by an officer of the law splashing into the estate's pool to rescue an innocent child. Hysteria and mayhem gripped the women who were supposed to be enjoying a vacation wedding with old college friends. Police called for backup and an ambulance. Taryn fainted into someone's arms. Sound, red darting color, and bright light from efficient flashlights cutting the dim mood of Manatee Moss Hidden Harbor's interior sent Laurel's brain into a dazed phase. She turned to Jackie with wide eyes and a loss for words.

"Come here," Jackie said, pulling Laurel into a soft, firm, comforting embrace, holding her in a true, solid, realistic place while the officers worked to revive young Patrick.

Chapter 15

Saturday morning dawned far too early for the group of friends. The medical examiner had taken Becky's body away in the night, confirming she'd died Wednesday evening, but unable to say what had been the cause of her death. No one wanted to believe Harmony had seen blood in the attic, least of all Harmony. The black bag that carried their friend away hid the evidence of anything terrible.

They didn't want to see anything terrible.

Laurel was asleep on the couch in the parlor when Marigold drove the four-door sedan back to the house, bringing Clara and Brad back from the hospital around daybreak. She stretched and moved to the front door to greet them.

Brad went straight to the kitchen, no doubt to open a beer. Clara turned to Laurel's arms for a hug and wept on her friend's shoulder, muttering her regret at allowing her children to come to this wedding, this vacation, this rotten house with its enticing dangers.

Marigold tossed the key fob that they'd retrieved from the attic the night before onto the dining room table. She massaged her temples as if she could smooth tension out of her head that way.

Taryn walked down the stairs with her tablet in hand. "Hey, guys. I thought I heard the car pull up."

"It's been a long night," Marigold said. "The police asked thousands of questions."

"About the pool?" Laurel asked. "That was an accident."

"Yeah, but they asked a lot of questions about Becky," Marigold pulled out one of the dining room chairs and took a seat, checking her gel manicure for damage. "It doesn't sound like they think she slipped and hurt herself up there."

"Um, I found some information," Taryn said. "It's kinda weird, but I think we're in the middle of *weird* right now."

Clara released Laurel to glare at Taryn. "You let my son drown and now you're talking about weird? You think this is *weird*? I'll tell you what's weird, young lady!"

"Okay, let's not get too—"

"No, Laurel, this stupid little imp let my child..." Clara choked on her words and her breath. "My little boy could have died."

Her tears came on fast and furious, punctuated by the sound of Brad slamming things around in the kitchen. Something in there broke; it sounded like something heavy going through one of the windows.

Laurel pulled Clara back into her arms while the bereaved mother shook with anger and sobs, and Marigold rose to stop Brad from losing their deposit on the house. The noise woke the rest of the friends and soon the group had gathered in a sort of quiet, commiserating therapy session in the parlor. Even Brad settled down once his daughter and father were situated quietly in their room upstairs and the rest of the friends wrapped their energy around one another.

What was supposed to be a happy, exciting weekend had been marred by accidents and tragedy. But Taryn thought she had an explanation for the strangeness around them, and she intended to share it.

"So-oh, I am by no means trying to minimize what's happened. Nearly losing a beautiful young boy is sad beyond words and I'm so so sorry that it happened. But Penny said something yesterday in the van and again last night that freaked me out, so I had to look into it. She talked about a man with ugly eyes. I mean, she blamed a man with ugly eyes for luring Patrick out to the pool. She said the man lives here and she said his picture is on the wall.

"Now, before Sue went missing, she talked to Marigold and to me about the pictures on the wall. She said they're weird because Native Americans didn't like to have their pictures taken. It was believed the photographer was taking your soul, or some such thing.

"These pictures are of Seminole Indians. Seminole is a Spanish word for *cimarron* and that means *runaway*. Runaways are what the different people who joined together in this area were called or were known for. Listen to this. I've got the 'Orlando Sentinel' page up here."

She read directly from the website: "During the next century, many escaped slaves found refuge among the Seminoles. Some slaves, known as Black Seminoles, stayed with the tribes permanently. But the white leaders of the United States were not pleased to see slaves being protected by and assimilated into American Indian tribes. In 1817, Andrew Jackson launched the first of three wars against the slave-harboring Seminoles. Peace did not come until 1842, when an agreement said several hundred members of the tribe could remain in Florida."

She looked at the group members to make sure she had their attention. "This whole area in Crystal River was a meeting place for rituals and burials of all kinds of Native Americans. They all came here, including Seminoles."

"I think you have bits and pieces of history all mixed up," Jackie said. "Native Americans were populating this area long before 1817 or 1842 or even 1776."

"Yes, but that's my point. This archeological zone is where people came to bury their dead. We're practically sitting on Indian burial grounds."

"Are you trying to tell us Patrick is on life support, Becky is dead, and Sue may be dead as well, because of Indian ghosts?" Kandy asked. They could all hear the rising anger in her voice.

"Don't be mad," Taryn said. "Just think about it. Think about it for a minute."

"Or maybe Florida just has the highest rate for drowning deaths of children in the United States," Marigold said.

"And how do you know that?" Brad asked.

"It's a fact," she said. "I live here, and I hear about it. Every spring we get the lectures and safety spiels from the news stations that the number of children who drown every year in this state could fill three or four preschool classrooms. We have building codes that boggle the mind just to keep kids from sneaking into pools. The latch on the back door?" Marigold gestured with her thumb toward the lanai in the back. "It's designed to stop kids who are Patrick's height from getting out there. The fact that he was able to get out the door last night is crazy."

They were all quiet for a moment.

"You knew this information and didn't warn us that our child could become a statistic?" Brad asked.

"What? I knew this and I knew all the safety devices are in place. Look at the fence around the lanai around the pool. Look at the latches on the guards. Look at the—"

"Enough!" Clara yelled. "Enough. I know these latches are there to keep children off the lanai. But if all these safety devices were in place, how did my son get in the water? No one opened the door for him. He's three years old. He can't open that door by himself with that latch on it. I saw it. I know what it's for."

Taryn set the tablet on the end table beside her and said, softly, "The man with the ugly eyes opened it for him."

Chapter 16

Exhausted, many of the group members took naps instead of going on that day's planned outing. Clara sat dejectedly at the dining room table, holding Penny on her lap. Surprisingly, the five-year-old remained calm, still, almost dejected, and willing to sit quietly with her worried mother. When Laurel joined the two, she brought a new box of tissues from the downstairs bathroom for her.

"Thank you," Clara said softly.

"You're welcome. Tell me what else I can do for you."

"Nothing. There's nothing to be done. I've called my sister in Oklahoma and she's contacting the rest of the family for me."

Penny finally wiggled. "May I go watch TV?"

Clara hugged her and kissed the top of her head. "Yes. But be careful."

"I won't talk to any strangers. I promise."

As the little girl pattered away across the hardwood floor, Laurel leaned forward on the table. "Clara, you don't believe there's an evil man haunting this house, do you?"

"I don't know."

"Your daughter's safe. We're all keeping an eye out for strangers. No one's gonna grab her."

"I don't know. I'm waiting for Brad so we can go back up to the hospital to sit with Patrick."

Jackie came into the room with a small trash can and began gathering up the soggy, used tissues from around Clara. "Can I bring you some water? Some tea?"

"No, thank you. There's nothing to be done."

Brad clomped down the stairs and looked in the dining room. "I can't find the blue tie you packed for me. Did you put it in a drawer?"

Clara stared at him as if not understanding the question.

"My blue tie," he repeated.

"Surely you're not going to the rehearsal dinner," Jackie said.

"I am. And so is Clara. And so is Penny."

Clara put her head down on the table.

"I think that's asking a bit much of yourselves," Laurel said. "You've just had an enormous tragedy. Clara thought you were getting ready to go back to the—"

"You think I don't know that? Look, sitting here crying isn't waking my son up. We have to eat, and the meal is free, so we're going to the rehearsal dinner as planned, and we're going to be perfectly delightful guests. Clara, where the hell is my blue tie?"

~ ~ ~

As a member of the wedding party, Marigold was *required* to attend the rehearsal. The rest of the out-of-town guests were invited to the rehearsal dinner at The Plantation on Crystal River.

"We should have stayed here," Jackie mused, lifting a fruity drink to her lips. Laurel sat beside her at the hotel's bar while they waited for the guests to be called in for dinner.

The banquet room had been reserved for the event and hotel staff were putting on the finishing touches while the wedding party arrived. A worker wearing an aquamarine cumber bund hustled past with a bouquet of aquamarine and slate gray roses exploding from a flat vase. No doubt a last-minute centerpiece with the bride's colors was about to be placed to perfection as if no one in Citrus County had died while vacationing for the event.

"Those roses remind me of your eyes," Laurel said.

Jackie's cheeks flushed a bit at the unexpected compliment, and she smiled. "Yeah, we should've stayed here. You and me. No alcoholics making things tense. No friends going missing. No sweet little kids falling into pools."

It had taken a Herculean amount of energy for the friends to get themselves dressed for the evening and put on forced smiles. At one point, Laurel wondered if her face looked as plastic as it felt. Too many pictures were going to show her with the same expression of fake pleasantness, fake cheer. Too many pictures were going to show her hoping the camera wasn't stealing her soul.

Before the dinner started, she walked out to the pineapple-shaped fountain to make a wish. She held a quarter in her hand, closed her eyes, and thought about what she wanted most from the next two days. To find Sue safe and sound, wandering around communing with nature and spirits? To see Patrick wake up fully restored to perfect health? Or mere survival?

When she opened her eyes, she looked at the quarter in her hand and decided she was better off keeping the twenty-five cents. She put it back in the pocket of the sleek and silky one-piece jumpsuit she wore tonight and returned to the bar.

During the meal, she and Jackie were seated at a table with Brad, Clara, Penny, Mr. Brandon, and a couple from the groom's side of the family. Small talk came slowly, painfully. Clara, understandably, had her thoughts somewhere else, and downed pain pills with several glasses of wine, effectively silencing her in a drowsy, almost catatonic state.

Laurel felt sorry for the husband and wife duo who tried but couldn't get conversations started with the little family. The conservative husband finally attempted to speak to the lesbians. Jackie snickered at him.

"Yes, we came in Wednesday afternoon," Laurel answered. "We've known Jen since college. And did you all know Jen before the engagement?"

The couple looked relieved for an exchange of words. "Um, no," the man said. "Jeremy is my cousin, and we live in different states, so...this is the first time we're meeting Jen. She seems wonderful."

"She's a true friend," Laurel said.

"True blue," the wife chimed in, pointing at the teal napkin by her plate. "Everything for the wedding is such lovely blue."

All the ladies smiled politely at the conversation-killing observation.

"I'm gonna visit the bar," Brad said.

Chapter 17

By the time they got home, two of them had to help Brad stumble into the house. He couldn't possibly make it up the stairs, so they deposited him on one of the couches in the parlor. Clara sat next to him, speaking quietly about something Laurel couldn't hear. She would have been surprised to hear Clara suggesting Mr. Brandon had fallen asleep in the van, but Clara didn't have the energy to drag the poor old man into the house. She would *not* have been surprised to hear Brad say, "let him sleep out there."

Taryn threw her shoes and purse in her room and came back down with her phone. "Okay. So-oh, who wants to look at pictures from the evening? I mean, that'll be cheery. Right?"

Laurel reached for Jackie's hand too late. She was scooting up the stairs and away from the situation.

"I think that would be nice," Harmony said. "And when Marigold gets back, we can see pics she took at the rehearsal."

"Exactly!" Taryn said. "That's the spirit." She was busily hooking up the TV and changing the inputs and channels.

"I think I'll just get some sleep," Kandy said. "The wedding's gonna seem really early tomorrow."

"That's because you drank so much tonight," Laurel teased her.

"Pfpfuhk jhou," Brad slurred.

"She's not talking to you," Clara said.

"You know, I could make a pot of coffee," Laurel suggested.

"Let me help you," Clara said, moving slowly, but forcing herself to move.

While they went to the kitchen, Harmony slipped out to the bathroom, leaving Taryn and Penny with Brad. Taryn looked down at the little girl who stood next to her in front of the television. "Ready to see how pretty you look in your dress?"

The girl nodded.

"Okay...here...is...here!" Taryn brought the first image onto the TV screen. "There's your mom in the background on this one. This is our friend Jen right here with Laurel."

"I know who Jen is," Penny said.

"Okay, Miss Knowitall, who's this person?"

Penny squinted at the dark shape at which Taryn pointed. Both Penny and Taryn tilted their heads as if to see the man better. From his place on the couch, Brad snorted a laugh at them. To him, they looked like puppets moving in unison. He closed his eyes to ignore them better.

As Penny began her answer, Taryn gasped. She couldn't believe what she saw on the screen, what her phone had captured, not in black and white, but in full color muted by shadows.

"That's the man with the ugly eyes," Penny said. "The man that the old lady works for."

Taryn looked down at her phone where the shape of the man moved behind Clara on the small screen. The fact that the figure moved startled her.

This wasn't video. He shouldn't have been moving. She swiped left to change the picture.

"There he is again," Penny said.

This time, the man appeared larger, closer to the camera, and was not as darkened by shadow. His vivid red sash and headband showed up better this time, as did the dark ink around his eyes.

"Oh my God," Taryn said. "But he wasn't even there. I never took that man's picture."

She swiped left to change the picture again and the man's horrible, scarred face filled both screens.

Taryn let out a yelp as the man's eyes and mouth opened wide. Opened wide to expose red where the whites of his black eyes should have been. Opened wide to expose black where the pink of his tongue should have been. Opened wide to expose pointed teeth that looked as if they'd each been sharpened by inaccurate blows of heavy, breaking stones.

Taryn cringed against the pain of an invisible claw grabbing her around her neck. She could feel some physical pressure pushing into her brain as if she'd been plunged into the ugliness on the glass before her.

She tried to scream for help, but no sound came out of her. Her body lunged forward as if another claw grabbed her waist and pulled her through the plasma screen. She was pulled into the scene and hung there, suspended in the space of a shutter-snap within the rehearsal dinner memories as if this was the true reality.

Taryn blinked at the people in the image beside her, her mind trying to grasp the inability to move, the inability to change this. She stood next to a drowsy looking Clara in the picture, merely a set of pixels waiting for someone to notice and help her.

Brad startled awake and grumbled at Penny: "Stop making so much noise."

Kandy walked into the room as Penny picked up the phone from the floor.

"Are you okay, sweetie? Did you yell?"

"No. Taryn did." Penny handed the phone to the adult.

"Where is she?"

Penny pointed at the TV screen where the rehearsal dinner scene froze in utter stillness. Taryn stood next to Clara in the picture and to Kandy, this made sense. Someone must have had Taryn's phone at some point in the evening to capture some special moments. Of course, Clara looked half asleep and Taryn looked punked out on cocaine.

"She looks kinda freaked out, doesn't she? She must not have been ready for the picture. Are there any pictures of you?"

"Probably."

Kandy swiped left on the phone's screen to get to the next image, which showed Clara in the background again, this time without Taryn. The picture changed simultaneously on the plasma TV.

"Who's the guy back there?" Kandy asked.

"You're so loud," Brad moaned.

Kandy ignored him, squinting at the image. "I don't remember a guy wearing that...is that canvas? Look at him."

"Don't look too close," Penny warned.

Kandy smiled at her. "Or?"

Penny lowered her voice in pitch and volume: "Or he might take you, too."

"What?"

"Coffee should be ready in a minute," Laurel announced. She stopped at the entrance to the parlor, aware that the vibe in the room wasn't right. "Kandy?"

"Do we know where Taryn is?" Kandy asked.

"She was setting up the pictures for us to view on the big screen," Laurel said.

"And now?" Kandy prompted.

"She's in the TV with the man," Penny said.

"Brad, where did Taryn go?" Laurel asked.

"I'm telling you," Penny said, "she went in the TV."

Brad moaned and muttered something about witches. He ended comparing his predicament with being in hell.

Kandy swiped the phone's screen right to go back to the previous picture. As the photo stopped on the small screen, and on the television in front of them, without Taryn, the man in the shadows lunged to the front of the image.

Penny screamed, flopping to the floor and scooting away from the television. The man's red and black eyes popped forward as his face and head seemed to explode from the plasma screen, real and solid, leading his body forward.

Brad started to complain, but the words stopped in his mouth as this new threat pounced into the room, onto the couch, and onto him. Now Kandy screamed, dropping the phone. Laurel reached out to pull Penny close to her body, close to where she could protect her.

The menace that had popped out of the television opened its ugly mouth to expose jagged, broken teeth, and closed its black lips down around Brad's throat. With a guttural roar, the creature ripped and tore the drunken man's throat open, yanking flesh, sinew, and bloody strips away.

Then he turned and locked his angry gaze with Laurel.

She put her hand over Penny's eyes and pulled the girl out of the room, through the foyer, toward the dining room. Too much was happening too quickly. Too much horrible evil that couldn't be real.

Behind her, Kandy screamed again, and the creature yanked its head around like an owl to face her. But Laurel wasn't waiting around to see if Kandy moved from her paralyzed place shrieking at the horror before her.

"Get out!" Laurel shouted to the rafters. "Get out! Get out of the house!" She dragged Penny toward the kitchen—where Clara stood with a look of utter confusion—and she yelled, "We've got to get out of here!"

"What's...Oh my God!"

The creature had followed, running behind Laurel. His mouth dripped blood down his chin and chest. Clara had no way of knowing that was her husband's blood, but she did know it was a bad omen.

The man with the ugly eyes had become real, not just a figment of Penny's imagination or Taryn's web research. And now he pulled a hatchet from his belt, raising it over his head as if he would butcher them crossing the threshold into the kitchen. With no other options immediately available, Clara grabbed the coffee pot and flung the boiling liquid in his face.

That worked for a moment. The being stopped moving forward, stopped gnashing his horrible teeth, stopped waving the hatchet, to scream and put his hands to his scalding skin.

Laurel shoved Penny into Clara's arms and tore open a drawer where the knives rested, waiting. No longer a peacekeeper, she pulled one out and turned to face nothing.

The man was gone.

"Where'd he go?" Laurel demanded.

Clara sobbed out, "he faded. He just faded."

"We're getting out of here," Laurel said. "Jackie!" she shouted.

Of course, Jackie had come back downstairs when the screaming began. Seeing blood and mangled people shook her from the lazy sleep she wanted to fall into. "What the hell?"

Laurel transferred the knife to her left hand and used her right to grab Jackie's arm. "We have to go. We're getting out of here."

"What? How?" Jackie's confused gaze grazed the bloodied footprints across the foyer, searching for something normal among the chaos. "Do we have keys for the van? Our stuff is upstairs."

"Jackie! This place lured us here to kill us. People are dying. We have to go. Screw our stuff."

"I second that!" Harmony called down.

"My purse," Jackie said. "I gotta have my license to get on a plane. How are we getting out of here without—"

"Are you listening to me?" Laurel shouted, shaking her firmly. The orders she now barked in an authoritative tone commanded the rest of her friends to action. "There is a supernatural being tearing peoples' throats out. We. Have. Got. To. Go."

Harmony limped across the landing upstairs. "I have your purse, too," she called down. "I'm comin'—"

Some kind of sick, gurgling, liquid sound cut her words short and the thumping, bumping sound of her body falling replaced her voice. She crashed part of the way down the staircase, head-first, with her arms instinctively trying to stop the fall.

Laurel ran up the few steps to Harmony's hands, grabbed Jackie's purse, and ran back down, looping the bag over the knife so she could keep one hand free.

Clara had the front door open, tripping from back pain as she dragged her daughter out of the manor, across the front porch. Laurel pulled Jackie right behind her. "Faster, Clara!" Laurel prodded her.

The four of them piled into the van, Clara started it, and peeled out. Mr. Brandon startled awake but didn't ask any questions. He looked nervous, as if he were in trouble, but Laurel shot a quick, reassuring smile at him before she yanked the side door closed. Jackie stammered something about being careful not to fall out of the van. Penny clicked her seat belt and announced, "The old lady!"

None of them wanted to see Mrs. Powell dealing with the mess they were leaving behind, but Laurel couldn't help following Penny's pointing finger back toward the front porch.

The aged woman stood in statuesque relief against the manor's dim interior lighting, merely watching them speed away. Light reflected off a metal blade in the woman's hand, but Laurel had no illusions of it being used for defensive purposes. Mrs. Powell was as much a part of the evil and horror at this estate as the creature that had taken her friends' lives.

Adrenaline sobered Clara, vibrating her muscles and masking any pain she'd been feeling. She shouted to Jackie in the passenger seat, "Guide me! Get me back to the Plantation!"

As Clara drove like a bat out of Hell down the gravel road, Laurel pulled her cell phone out of her pocket and pressed Marigold's name.

"Hey, Laurel," Marigold spoke brightly. "We're just about done here—"

"Do *not* return to the house. We're *never* come back to this place. We're coming to you."

The End

Epilogue

Sunday morning promised a lovely sunshiny day for Jen and Jeremy's wedding, whether all their friends would attend or not. Unknown to the happy couple, what few of Jen's friends were still alive were checking a three-year-old child out of the nearby hospital and driving out of the state in a rental van.

At the Manatee Moss Hidden Manor, a soft green two-door Roadster pulled onto the gravel parking area next to an Enterprise rental sedan, and a forty-something gentleman got out. He walked up to the antebellum house's beige front door and knocked. After a minute, the door opened, and Mrs. Molly Powell stood politely to the side with her grim smile.

"Ah, you must be Dorian," she said.

About the Author

Sandy Lender is a magazine editor by day and author of girl-power fantasy novels by night. "Destination Premeditation" is her first foray into the horror genre. Her successes include both traditionally and self-published novels; hundreds of magazine articles; multiple short stories in competitive anthologies; a first-place award for a sequel to Harper Lee's "To Kill a Mockingbird" during her high school days; APEX technical writing awards in 2016, 2017, and 2020; an IMADJINN 2019 Best Literary Fiction Novel Award for her #MeToo novel "She's Not Broken;" and a 2020 Pushcart Prize nomination for her short story "Woman off the Grid."

She lives in Florida where she volunteers in sea turtle conservation, parrot rescue, and dragon-whispering. With a four-year degree in English and twenty-eight-year career in publishing, Sandy brings a deep understanding of public relations and journalism to a variety of projects. She's beaten cancer twice, but still fights the IRS. You can check out her author page on Amazon or follow her facebook page at Fantasy Author Sandy Lender.

Other Works by Sandy Lender
The Choices Series
Choices Meant for Gods
Choices Meant for Kings
Choices Meant for All
What Choices We Made, Vol I
What Choices We Made, Vol II

The Dragons in Space Series
Problems on Eldora Prime
Problems above Pangaea Moon
Problems in Annady's Core

May Your Heart Be Light
We Can't Let You In, A Diary of the PyreDees Plague of 2016
She's Not Broken, IMADJINN 2019 Best Literary Fiction Novel
How to Train Your Human: A Guide for Parrots
Move the Stars
Poems of Trials, Triumphs, and Turtles
Destination Premeditation

Short Stories
"A Legacy Protected," *Winter's Night, Vol I*
"Desecrated Ring," Keith Publications Halloween
"Dragons in Crisis," *Winter's Night, Vol II*
"Perceptions on New Year's Eve," *A Yuletide Wish* Anthology
"Woman Off the Grid," *Wild Women* Anthology
"Della Finds Her Gift," TulipTree Genre Anthology
"Under the Ice"

Visit **www.SandyLenderInk.com**
Destination Premeditation
First edition copyright 2020

www.ingramcontent.com/pod-product-compliance
Lightning Source LLC
Chambersburg PA
CBHW020557130626
46552CB00007B/2927